T0147034

Strange Associations

Strange Associations

John M. Hill

STRANGE ASSOCIATIONS

iUniverse books may be ordered through booksellers or by contacting:

iUniverse
1663 Liberty Drive
Bloomington, IN 47403
www.iuniverse.com
1-800-Authors (1-800-288-4677)

ISBN: 978-1-5320-7271-0 (sc)
ISBN: 978-1-5320-7272-7 (e)

Print information available on the last page.

iUniverse rev. date: 04/16/2019

Contents

Prologue

The Waldorf Astoria hotel was just as I remembered it from the time in my late teens, while we nosed in for a peek when I was a guest visitor from Springhill, a small mining town in Nova Scotia, Canada, to the home of relatives of my girlfriend, in New York City. To be there at all, the glitter and glamour of the New Year's Eve ball in the Waldorf hotel was fantastic, even when viewed from the foyer, and the sea of revellers in Times Square was awesome. In that setting, Darlene was the most beautiful creature in both heaven and earth in her pale blue strapless gown that night, about three years before she died of an acute version of Parkinson's disease. As she was a twenty-nine year old divorcee, a nurse and airline stewardess, runner-up in the Miss Canada beauty contest (i.e. one of the most beautiful women in a country of 40 million); and because I was just an eighteen year old pharmacy student, she was my first 'Strange Association'. I loved that woman.

Ten years later, this "farm boy" was having luncheons in the same place it all started for me- the opulent ballroom of the Waldorf Astoria, with a Roche VIP at each table, and, being treated like royalty. It was another strange situation, for me at least.

This visit a decade later was on business, but very pleasant business indeed. As a three-year top sales representative of one of the largest pharmaceutical research companies in the world, I was invited to attend a combined Canada/ United States Sales Convention to be held for five days in Nutley, New Jersey, headquarters and research centre of Hoffmann-LaRoche (ROCHE) in the U.S.A. It was for the North American launch of Valium in1966. All of the invited Canadian sales representatives were quartered at the Waldorf hotel, as a reward for a great year, and my recent order for a million doses of Librium to one of my hospitals, had been a noticeable contributor to mine. The ten- hour days of intensive training and study in neuropharmacology, psychiatry, physiology, etc., allowed for minimal entertainment, but I made it to jazz clubs like the Blue Note, etc., my most preferred venue for jazz and swing music. I met Zoot Sims there, my favourite tenor sax player, and role model in my efforts with the saxophone.

For a few of the days, luncheons were held in the same ballroom as I had seen a decade earlier, at tables for ten, each table presided by a major executive or VIP from the facility in Nutley. For some of the luncheons I was seated beside a small, older, but very personable chap, who turned out to be the current Director of Research for Roche USA, and the chemist who invented the family of chemicals of which Librium was the first and most successful to date, and now Valium was the latest (yes, the Germans called it 'the drug of the valiant.'-??) We 'hit it off' and he started to tell me his story. The more he told me, the more fascinated I became, and, realising that, he decided to pour out the most unusual story I will ever hear, "even if I live to be a hundred" (and I'm 78 now). It took three lunches that went overtime and therefore some difficulty with my boss, but I think it was worth almost losing my job.

The research chemist wanted to make it clear that his pride and claim to fame was simply to have developed a carbon ring with an unusual configuration. Nature loves symmetry, and carbon rings normally have six sides, or eight once in a while. His achievement, according to him, was simply to have developed a five-sided configuration, which won him an obscure award at his university in Krakow, Poland, in the 1930's. He won a coveted ring from the university, which he later had to use as an engagement ring for his fiancé at the start of the war, as she was taken to the Warsaw Ghetto as a Jew, and he went after her.

During the conversations at the luncheon, he admitted that this discovery had changed his life greatly because the pharmacologic tests with his chemical, done by Roche, suggested that it had unusual effects like altering the effects of fear and anxiety on the body, and perhaps reducing fear itself. This caused him a "little trouble" when Nazi Germany learned of it, as did the Americans and British, as it became one of Hitler's touted "Secret Weapons", but in the end, Roche was able to rescue him and provide a safe haven during the war, and eventually a wonderful situation in the U.S.A. It was never established whether his drug or a placebo (dummy) was used by some Nazi S.S. Blitzkreig troops heading the invasions, but Hitler, historically, did use an "anti-fear drug" as one of his secret weapons at the start of the war, while the supply lasted. In my innocence, I commented later that his story would make a good book. Andre, my boss at the time, said, "Write it, and I will have to fire you, and sue you for all you're worth." Apparently, Roche had the usual Swiss attitude of requiring anonymity in all its dealings, even heroism, altruism, and developer of miracles. They are still doing this, and I may write a book about them some day, now that I'm retired.

The Author

Notice

This is inspired on a true story, this is a work of fiction, and all of the events and persons are fictitious. Names, when appropriate, have been changed to protect persons who may have been involved in some scenes or scenarios at a similar time or place.

Although the basic events and elements of this story are true, it is a work of fiction, and any similarity to any of the characters depicted is purely coincidental. Names, dates, and other items are purely fictitious, or have been changed for the protection of real persons when necessary. Let's face it, I was born the year before Germany overran Poland, so everything I know about the story has been related to me by others, however, I trust these sources. I have been in similar situations to those of the characters and have sometimes described how I would have reacted. I have been lucky in my life to be one of the few to have found my soul mate, so I can understand the thinking of the main characters. I hope you will approve of my ability to relate it.

I also may have a different opinion of the need for secrecy in EVERY action of my erstwhile employer, who (?) is the most secretly revered pharmaceutical research and manufacturing company in this world by both its competitors and customers, the physicians- even those who malign it, and the pharmaceutical industry, for their own purposes. So, sue me if you must, this story will be told!

The Author, John M. Hill

Dedicated to my soul mate, lover, and erstwhile fiancé, Ann Manzo, the model for "Fran", also lost to me forever. JMH

1

CAMP X: Prelude to Hades

RICK CARTER

The office of Colonel Bill Stephenson was Spartan, small, and belied his position as the top man of this international secret spy training agency, although Rick noticed two well worn overstuffed leather chairs looked more comfortable than anything he had encountered during his three-month training period, here in the middle of a Canadian wilderness, in northern Ontario. The wags had said that "Camp X" meant it had been crossed off years ago, and they had just forgotten to close it up. It was not near anything, but also not near good hunting or fishing, or any large town, but it was very well known by the RCMP, and even they had to have special clearance to enter a primary boundary, miles from the camp itself. It was one of those strange, double edged oxy-morons often used in security: It did not exist officially, and if it did, entrance was forbidden. Anyone thought to have talked about it was "examined" very carefully.

Colonel Stephenson had set this camp up and it was Spartan but comfortable. Trainees came from around the world, from British Commonwealth countries, and even from the United States, where the participation of that country in the war was in doubt, officially, at the time. Currently, the usual political confusion, and grab for power, was happening between the FBI and several other agencies, and a few wannabe ones, in the U.S., especially military.

When the colonel entered, Rick succumbed to the temptation to throw him a salute, even though he wasn't wearing a uniform. His military bearing and piercing, all encompassing glance, prompted it. "Belay that", he said with a smile. "That is one reaction you must lose while you're here, and even more so, afterwards."

Rick replied, "Leftenant Carter, reporting as ordered, sir." "Just call me Bill," Col. Stephenson ordered, "you're ex-FBI, and your only military connection is as a trainee of the Canadian Army commando unit. You can forget the salute but remember how to kill with your bare hands." With another smile, he said, "I wanted to discuss your assignment.

We operate on my 'need to know' basis, but I believe you need to know it all to succeed this time."

Rick decided this fellow was perhaps the perfect spy. Everything about him was normal or average: height about 5'10", lean and fit, but projecting a careless attitude about his persona, dark hair- cut not too short, hard, black eyes, hidden by humorous eyebrows and an easy smile. As he started into the assignment, he leaned slightly forward and raised his eyebrows as one would when telling a joke.

"There is a chemist in Poland who developed a new series of chemicals, one of which seems to have an effect on fear. The Nazis are hot on his trail, and we must find him before they do. They may have already used this drug on their SS 'shock troops' at the beginning of the war, but somehow seem to have lost track of him and his drug. It may be one of the "Secret Weapons" Hitler has been talking about."

"Damn, that's interesting." Rick thought, out loud, he asked, "Do we know where he is?"

Stephenson continued, "He disappeared a few months ago in Krakow, but one of our people believes he saw him in Warsaw, in the Ghetto" "Ghetto?" Rick asked.

Stephenson paused, then proceeded in a sad, reflective tone, "One of the first things the Nazis did after overrunning Poland, was to round up all the Jews in Warsaw and move them to an old section of the city and set up guards and check points. They plan to wall it off. They now seem to be gathering Jews, as well as people with "Jewish names" but without papers, from all over the country, and interning them in the "Jewish neighbourhood". It's like a big prison, well guarded but without provisions.

They will let many of them starve or die of disease until they figure out an easier way of eliminating them, as part of Hitler's plan for solving the "Jewish problem".

Rick grunted, "So the rumours are true then, but worse. Who would have thought that would happen in 1939? Sounds like it will be easy to get in, but a problem getting back out-with another in tow. Will he come willingly?"

Under hooded eyelids, Col. Stephenson replied with passion close to anger, "It is essential that we recover him intact and bring him to North America under protection. He may still be the only person who can produce his chemical. The Germans seem to have run out of their supply and are trying hard to find him. Now we have information that he went into Warsaw to find his fiancé, and is probably not a recorded resident of the ghetto; she is, however. If it is not possible to get him out, for <u>any</u> reason, then he must die. Understand?

Rick nodded, "and we should start quickly!"

"Yes. The assignment is code named "ECHO" and you will ultimately report to me. You will have full authority and responsibility, but you will be briefed and equipped by the British MI, and then assisted by what's left of the Polish underground resistance. Your plane to England leaves in one hour." And then with a sincere salute, "Good luck!" Stephenson has the ability to put tons of sincerity and hope into those last words, Rick thought, and a good smile besides. Here is a good man. "Thank you, I'll need it." He said. Yes, I'll need luck, and lots of it. I have learned to fly, parachute, navigate, write and think in codes, and kill (theoretically only-and that's something to worry about. Can I really kill if I have to? Will I know when I have to? Etc.)

On his way back to his barracks, he had a lot to think about, 'Here I am, Rick Carter, a simple pharmacist who got involved with the F.B.I. to help identify illicit narcotics, then enforce the relative laws, then help with several good arrests, even going undercover for a good conviction, the highpoint before the war. But now, I am learning to kill with my bare hands, all the spy trade, and about to parachute into Poland, or somewhere behind enemy lines, wherever they are currently. Life takes such strange twists, and associations." He thought about this well into the night, and only slept after a good scotch.

DARIUS KUNZ

Darius Kunz came away from his meeting with the Polish chemist feeling a bit let down, depressed even. 'I did not accomplish anything positive', he thought, 'he doesn't think his discovery is very important, even though his peers have just awarded him a medal, or at least a ring. I showed him the data we have on the prototype sample, especially the pharmacologic and toxicologic tests: No significant effect on vital organs, vital signs in humans normal with only a slight reduction in blood pressure, no long term effect on animals, low potential for dependence or addiction, but "fight or flight" parameters changed more specifically than with phenobarbital or meprobamate. He had never heard of fight or flight, which was described by our people and documented in all the journals ever since we developed the first antidepressant, a MAOI inhibitor, "Marsilid". (It is always a bit strange the way things happen: Roche was working with its anti-TB drug "Rimifon"- and after finding a better chemical relative with at least the same effectiveness with better tolerance; after testing in humans found that they had-to a man- an improved mood), this by changing from isoproniazid to iproniazid. Back to "Librium" and the chlordiazepamoxide molecule, not even serious drowsiness, unless you go to the nitrate end of the line of analogs like nitrazepam.

He seems to have no interest in brain chemistry. I covered all the elements, but the damn missing carbon is only significant in the theoretical sense. He really believes he has had an epiphany in theoretical chemistry similar to Einstein's theory as epiphanies go. Of course, he doesn't know or care about Poulenc's work on phenothiazines. Heck, he doesn't care at all about pharmacology, even generally. 'I get all the weird ones.'

'In fact, his concern for his girlfriend, just a Jewess, seems to have clouded his judgement and added to his unassuming nature. Damn eggheads,' he thought, 'when I write my report I will suggest that his promise to "think about it" is really a promise to forget it. What more could he want? Other chemists would give their right arm for the salary and laboratory I offered. He just needs to move to Switzerland, which is going to be neutral in this mess. He wants to bring his girlfriend! I even agreed to that!' What else is there?

'However, in the final analysis, I failed. I must continue to press him. Something will work: Maybe more money? Damn!'

After sequestering himself in his hotel room, with a nice glass of cold vodka on one side of the desk and a small schnapps on the other for balance, Darius took a deep breath and picked up his pen. 'This report must be able to send the right message: not too enthusiastic, somewhat hopeful but reserved for next time. There must be another meeting. Reports are so much easier when the facts speak for themselves. You just finish with a conclusion and file it. No problem!' he mused to himself.

'Do I have any solid facts this time? We met and talked about his medal, which he doesn't believe he deserves. The ring would have been enough. He is very unassuming and nondescript, about 5'8", grey hair and moustache –looking kind of "Einstein-ish", as is common these days. He is impressed with our offer of a good salary, and, more important, his own lab, but he is more concerned with his woman: her well-being and safety, and whether she would, or could, move into Switzerland. He seems unaware that any group-much less country- would become interested in him. I'm sure that he has not been in direct contact with German chemists. He did not even know about Hoechst Chemik-Fabrik. One thing is for certain: I must get him, with or without his girlfriend, over my country's border before it is closed to Jews or Polish nationals, or anyone. Neutrality is always difficult to gain, and even worse to maintain, so he cannot take too long to "think it over".'

"Why me?" He commiserated with himself, "I was hired by this company when it was just a big drugstore after the war in the late 'teens, expanding when they secured a corner on opium alkaloid production by inventing a way of extracting them from the raw stuff. I was a history teacher hired to write about one of the founders, a woman named Francesca Hoffmann, their main chemist. I was supposed to go back to teaching, but instead I got married twice while travelling and luckily the first died before the bigamy was found out, only then could I stop travelling but then I didn't because Roche wanted to expand, and I liked the life of a variety of sex partners. When I looked at it from that perspective, I was not surprised at the variety of strange associations."

HEINRICH SCHLAGER

Heinrich Schlager was becoming irritated with Bruno and Dieter, his heavy-handed assistants. They were making too much noise smashing equipment and painting swastikas on the blackboards of this "citadel of Jewish intelligentia", the main chemistry laboratories of the University of Krakow. Granted, they were doing a good job of showing that this lab had been visited by the Brown shirts as a general warning that Jews were not welcome here, or anywhere else, for that matter. As simple labourers, both had an inferior education and with it a child-like glee in destroying the glassware and machines they did not understand. Their ignorant, generalised destruction provided a good cover for his project, however, which was to take all notes, samples, and whatever he could find about the assistant professor's chemical discovery, now code-named "FEARLESS" in mis-spelled German. "Why not just capture the man and remove him to Germany, if he is so important? This is 1939, not '33, and we have control!" he mused, "It would have been easier and perhaps more effective than this. Just call him a Jew, whether he is or not, to avoid repercussions. Sometimes I wonder about Herr Himmler – he may be less smart than he believes."

"So this is my army:" he thought, as he searched through the myriad of closets and drawers in this old laboratory, reading every scrap of paper, note books, and labels, hoping to find anything which may be of value. "Two lunkheads wearing the pre-war colours of the citizen's branch of the Nazi party in Poland. Good cover, though, the Polish police were told to look the other way and don't question them, although they can't be trusted, most are still loyal to Poland." "My army," he muttered to himself, "and me an officer of the Stueben Strasse, although in truth, I have been passed over so many times that I feel two centimetres tall. Maybe when the Blitzkreig troops take the country over officially next month, I will start moving up the ladder. I have been a good, loyal, party member for nearly seven years now, yeah, seven years in September. But anything is better than the clerk's job I had before." 'I wonder if that fool in England is appeasing to play for time? Everyone knows we are coming, are they trying to delay until the winter starts? This month the weather has been great, things get slowed down in winter. If I don't make kapitan this year, I will have to change my plans and career."

"Bruno!" he called, "Keep quiet now, and help me with this container, it must weigh ten or twenty kilograms. Be careful, I think this is everything that I came for. Don't drop it. Help him, Dieter, the Polish police may be coming."

Back in his room he called his superior. "Hello, Herr Lieutnant, I recovered a good quantity of sample and a drawer full of notes. Shall I bring them to you? Very good, then. I will wait here. Shall I continue to follow the chemist? O.K. then, the other project is as urgent, I agree. I will start early tomorrow. Very well (Jahwohl!). Heil to the Third Reich!

Our Hero...

As he surveyed the damage to his laboratory, Petr Chetovsky felt fear for the first time, more for his lovely assistant and fellow student Fran, than for himself. Professor Herz was right. He had warned him that too many questions were coming from Germany, and a "Brown shirt" was noticed hanging around the chemistry building. "They are too excitable," he thought, "those Germans don't even understand my work, much less organic chemistry in general. All that was published were some basic toxicity tests on my sample in rats, and just a few of them showed fearless behaviour before being sacrificed for autopsy. I wish that pharmacologist had not published his footnote."

"Fran has not arrived yet. She will be shocked at the mess, and we will have to start making more sample immediately. HLR Pharma wanted it for next week. I wonder if that will get me enough money to take her somewhere safe? She doesn't look like a Jewess; she has the most beautiful dark blue eyes and such a pretty face framed with the blonde hair, like the picture of her Scottish grandmother. God, I love that woman! I don't care about her faith, but I wish she had not been so blatant about it recently. Maybe they are after her only! I will propose marriage to her tonight, even though I have no money for a ring and haven't yet received her father's blessing. With my name she would be safe; and I would be in heaven.

"It is amazing how the world is changing for me. Nothing had ever happened here at the university, or for that matter, Krakow, and certainly not like this! It is just a quiet university town in a quiet area of Poland. Now, the Nazis have wrecked my lab and our police have to be uninterested, according to my friend at the station. I will have to call Mr. Kunz. I have a contract now with Roche to expand my research and development, and my lab has been ransacked. I have associations and relationships suddenly with a huge international corporation and with people I would never have had any connection with, even when I was younger, ..it is strange."

"Also," he mused, while he waited for the police, "I have a foreboding feeling that it isn't over. There is a war starting, everybody knows that, and it will be a big one. Hitler wants a new Aryan race in the whole world, Stalin wants more land and power, Italy and Japan have similar agendas, the United States is coming out of hiding, and Britain is worried about protecting what is left of its empire. Yes, it will be a big one, and maybe long.

Everyone's life will be changed, not just mine. Everyone will meet a stranger, maybe several, something we are not used to, at least not in this part of the world. We will make many strange associations with lots of different people. We will fight some, kill some, befriend some, love some,..... Oh, hi Fran, we have been ransacked."

"Oh, God, no!" "Why?......What?....Who did this? All our work, gone! I didn't think it would come to this. Do you think it was really Nazis?" She said, worriedly, "Maybe some students having fun? Or some hoodlums? The swastikas don't lie, they are serious!" She answered herself and slumped her shoulders in defeat. She searched for a broom, saying, "Can we save anything?"

"No," Petr said, "They took our sample, a month's work just making it. We have little time to make more, even if we had the equipment. It's disgusting. But we must try, I hope mister Kunz will understand. Let's get to work."

2

KRAKOW; Escape

Darius Kunz cursed mildly to himself as he replaced his telephone on its hook. "I don't need a setback, dammit," he thought, "according to her, they will need another month to rebuild the lab and reproduce the sample amount the Nazi's took (if, in fact, it was the Nazis- they are getting the blame for everything these days). I don't have a month, maybe not even a week, before they close the border. I suppose I should go over there and commiserate with them over the damage. It's probably just some hoodlums making a statement."

"On the other hand," he considered," that lab assistant sounded nice, even sexy, and she sounded familiar with the project. I think I'll go over there and try to meet her. She may also be a way to influence Petr, especially if she is his girlfriend. I have more sway with women than men anyway, especially if they're wives or fiancés. There is nothing more satisfying than turning the head of a beautiful, but attached, woman, and melting her to do anything I want in bed. She might bring him with her over the border and give me pleasure as well." he thought, cupping his balls with his hand.

Not one, but two police cars were parked in front of the Dultz residence, in this quiet, upper class neighbourhood of Krakow, an unheardof event causing great interest and disquiet among the neighbors, not because of the crowd of onlookers milling around, because there wasn't one. A sign of the times, the street was empty, a poignant sign that something very serious was happening, and, even more poignantly, the entire neighbourhood knew what was wrong, or at least the cause of this visit, by two police cars!

Actually, some neighbors with a vantage point to the rear became aware of a third, unmarked car parked strategically to cover rear exits from the Dultz residence. The occupants were not wearing the uniforms or the unique cap of the police force of Krakow, nor the usual dress of the national police, either. All were wearing the same shade of brown shirts, with darker splotches under the arms, from the summer heat hitting record temperatures this summer in 1939.

The Dultz family were Jewish, and proud of it, although mother and daughter appeared to be Aryan, with blonde hair and fair skin. They were the only Jewish family in the neighbourhood and were well accepted by most, and maybe tolerated by only a few. It would be difficult to pinpoint any of the neighbours who would complain overtly about this quiet, but friendly and helpful family. The father ran a good men's clothing store downtown, and their daughter was finishing university as a chemist. Yes, the only reason for a serious police visit would be that they are Jews and have not tried to hide it, as is usual these days. Rumour has it that several Jewish families have been accused of sedition or hatemongering and have been forced to move to a Jewish neighbourhood in Warsaw.

Oh, oh, there is the father now, carrying two suitcases, and they look heavy. You would think that one of the big, burly policemen would help the old man, who is at least going to need help putting the cases into the trunk, or perhaps having a heart attack trying. That would, of course, come under the category of helping a Jew, against one of the new unwritten laws from Germany, and the most inhuman and insane so far. Here comes his wife, and her heart is already broken, with tears streaming down her face, also struggling with an overstuffed suitcase and a large handbag. The daughter must be at work.

Fran Dultz is my assistant, as assistant professors are in this university, but she is much more, he thought, looking at the helpless and dejected look on her face, what an almost saintly beautiful woman, looking around at the damage to their laboratory. "My God I love her," he thought to himself, "she is so lovely."

"Yes, she was Jewish, but her looks belied that amazingly, her Scottish grandmother must have had strong genes." He described her to himself,

"She is so beautiful, with slightly strawberry blonde hair and blue eyes, looking as Aryan as they come, but with only a little bit turned up nose and not pale, but more swarthy and smooth, naturally unblemished, skin. She was taller than most at 110 cm. (5'7") and had a slightly larger than average bust, narrow waist (aided by the Polish strict rationing), and slightly smaller than normal hips-but not too much so for childbearing-long, well shaped legs, even without high heels,-legs which moved, when she walked, with a provocative rhumba or samba beat." He almost thought out loud: "So I love her even more, as she is my pin-up and her picture would be in the cockpit of my plane, if I was a flier." Petr returned to her description," An obviously happy and even- tempered lady, she laughed a lot, beautifully, and only stopped when the subject of race was brought up." The phone ringing broke his reverie:

While she spoke in the telephone, he muttered, "This is going to be a long job," he said, as he started to clean up, "they spilled the basic high Ph solvent, it's mixing with spilled oil and congealing to a kind of soap. Helluva way to help clean up." He quipped, then…

"My God, they got the sample!"

Fran Dultz hung up the phone with a frown and, turning to Petr said, "That was from a neighbour. My parents were arrested! They were given a half hour to pack and are being sent to Warsaw!" "Goodness," he said, "what for? They can't do that! They…." He closed his mouth and looked bleakly around the room; at the wreckage, the swastikas, the threats. "I'm so sorry, darling. We must hide you immediately. Let's get away from here!"

After a few minutes in the car, Fran calmed down, wiped her tears, checked her makeup, and blew her nose. "I can't go home, or they'll arrest me, too. But I must go directly to Warsaw, they must be scared silly!" Petr didn't dare say what was on his mind: "She and they would not be in trouble now if she had been quieter about her heritage. Even her parents were not as blatant as she, and went about their business quietly, not even having an obviously Jewish name. We all have been ignoring the poison Hitler has been spitting out."

Petr grunted, "I think we are being followed by that small, black Mercedes. I don't think it's police, but how can I find out? They don't usually use a Mercedes, and I can't imagine the goons owning one, either. I wonder if Herman is on duty at the police station. He would be discreet, but perhaps he could scare off whoever that is. I have my papers with me, do you? On second thought, try not to use yours. Maybe if we pull up in front of the station, our follower might lose interest."

Getting out of the car, he recognised Mr. Kunz getting out behind him. "So, it is you, Herr Kunz; you gave me a scare. I didn't recognise your automobile!" "Good morning, your assistant called me, are you having trouble?"

"Our laboratory has been raided, and equipment was destroyed, my sample was stolen, there are Nazi swastikas and Jewish threats everywhere! "He nodded Fran's way, "Now her parents have been taken away, and…….."

As Petr started to describe today's trouble, Darius cut him off and suggested, "We can't stop here for long. Why not follow me to my hotel and talk about it over some refreshment?"

"Very good. You go on ahead, and I'll follow you. Alright with you, Fran?" He said as he ran to the car.

The bar at the hotel was closed, but the concierge recognised Mr. Kunz as a frequent guest, and opened it himself, finding him a private table in a quiet corner on which he placed a bottle of Darius' favourite schnapps and some glasses.

"Both of you should come with me to Switzerland immediately. I've heard rumours the border from Poland will soon be closed, even to Polish nationals."

Petr bristled, "What do you mean, 'Polish nationals'? We are all Polish nationals!"

Darius tried to placate, but remain firm, with his advice. "I'm very sorry, but they seem to be considering Jews as foreigners, or at least non-citizens." "The Germans are preaching that kind of lie here, and too many are believing it. Not in Switzerland, of course. You would be safe there." He said, looking from one to the other to emphasize that both would be safer and more contented.

Fran Dultz finally joined the conversation. With a look of fear in her eyes, but determination on her face, she said, "I must find my parents. I must try to get them to a safe place, mother is not well. Father may not stand the strain!"

Darius thought, "This is the moment of truth. I must sell them on going to Switzerland, and now! If they get to Warsaw, they could be lost…..

or get lost,....or lose their life, even. She is as important to us as he is. She has been preparing the sample and working beside him for years and knows everything. Even if he stayed with me and they split up it would be no good. If I lost control of either one of them, the other might be found by Hoechst or Poulenc, or any of the others, if they survived this stupid war. Yes, I must do all I can to keep them together and get them to Basle, immediately."

He looked at this very pretty woman for a few seconds too long, and then considered, "It's a shame too, she is gorgeous, with my favourite kind of figure – not too heavy on top (they've been called 'perky'), but her waist and below draws me like a huge magnet; a target not easily avoided. Better not try her, at least not now, until they are secured, maybe even married. It's a shame, because I need her tonight......."

Out loud, he said, "If you would come with me and trust me, I would get you over the border quickly to safety and a great situation for yourselves, and then I would go to Warsaw to find them, myself. I know a lot of people and have contacted many officials in my work. Perhaps I could arrange for some kind of Swiss diplomatic protection for them, but things are changing fast, so we must hurry. Will you come now?"

Fran was looking at him and frowning in concentration, "I really don't trust him," she thought, "he was looking at me in not a good way. Some men look at you, and through you, but not into you."

"He would probably get us to Switzerland safely, but then he would try harder to get me in bed, than to try to get mama and papa out of Warsaw." An opinion he agreed with.

"Who knows? Maybe my parents would be happy in Warsaw, especially if this Nazi thing blows over." She thought out loud. "Surely this horrible German invasion will be stopped, and we can return to sanity." She said out loud.

To Darius Kunz she said, "I appreciate your offer, Herr Kunz, and I'm very grateful, but I think I should go directly to Warsaw and find them before something worse happens to them."

"If you go, I go," Petr said, "they are probably searching for you at this very moment, and perhaps they are looking for a single woman. I was going to propose marriage to you tonight, even though I had not discussed it with your father. It seems I have no time left to do anything right."

"Will you? I love you very much, you know."

Fran frowned, "I wonder if those men in brown shirts are looking for us. They seem to be threatening the concierge."

Darius glanced around, then stood up abruptly, saying, "Let's leave through this back door, just in case."

Outside, no one appeared to be watching as the fugitives ran to their car, loudly whispering to Darius, "We will either contact you directly, or your company, as soon as possible. Thanks for your help!"

Darius's car was the last to go, and in another direction. As he sped off, the brown shirts spotted him as they ran into the street, pointing at him and yelling at each other.

He spent the next hour making sure they had lost him, and then spent the next twenty-four hours changing hotels discretely, retrieving his belongings, and searching for a plan to change to. "What a mess." He thought.

He was no happier about the situation that night when he reported by telephone back to Basle. His only option would be to follow them to Warsaw and find them through the friend from whose apartment they had called on their arrival. Even the call had not been great; the fool really did not understand how important his discovery had been pharmacologically. His only interest was chemistry, and its intellectual borders were his horizon. To make matters worse, as he began to think out loud, "If I were to convince him of how valuable we think it is, his price would probably go up, so I must back off. Perhaps, when I call Basle they might have lost interest. The final toxicology reports should be in. A few dead mice would save me a lot of trouble!" and, with a change of subject, but not aloud, "Her sex appeal would go unattained, but there is lots of that here." he observed, giving the pretty hotel desk clerk one of his slow, lingering looks. She was still smiling at him and flicking her hair, as he asked her to place his call to Switzerland.

3

WARSAW: Escape to Hell

Andre Grolimond was mildly irritated when the international operator announced Darius Kunz' call. To himself, "He's a day late in calling, and he's still in Poland. Doesn't he know how urgent this project is?" then into the 'phone, "Hello, Darius. Why are you still there? It's now urgent that we have the chemist here, and bring his assistant, even if you have already had her in bed!"

"I'm fine, thank you," Darius answered wryly,"...and how is your health and happiness, old friend? We have a delay here, I think I had the chemist ready to come yesterday, but his assistant, his fiancé now, decided to go chasing after her parents who were arrested by the police. They're Jews you know, but she doesn't look it. They are somewhere in Warsaw, and I have to go after them. What can I arrange for them all if I can get them to the border?"

Andre took a deep breath and decided to tell all: "Darius, it is critical that you get them here safely and quickly. Spare no expense. Bring the parents and anyone else you need to, and quickly! This damn war is getting bigger every day, but our people have some special arrangements with the Pope, and maybe even Hitler, so we'll be neutral through this, I hope. Also, the Americans want him, I don't know why, but the code word is 'ECHO', if you ever need it."

Andre continued "Toxicology tells us that is the safest drug we have ever worked with, even safer than dextromethorphan, knock on wood. The effects of the drug on a new part of the brain called the limbic system are amazing! One of our guys, a neurophysiologist, discovered this circuit that controls the emotional side of life, and how the body is influenced by it. This chemical dampens a site called the amygdala and stimulates the hippocampus. Look it up after he publishes his paper when the war is over. We need more sample yesterday, for testing on humans. The destruction of his laboratory and sample by the 'brown-shirts', set us back about half a year. Our pharmacologists are even trying to extrapolate the animal test results. We need more sample, we need him, and we need to secure the process. Understand?

Poulenc are ahead of us with their phenothiazines, which they will try to market into the potential market of your chemical in spite of the difference, but Hitler has them shut down for now. Whoever is first, wins, you know; and we have always been first!"

"Next time you call, ask for my boss. I'm going to America to work on some expansion plans in a place called Canada, with our sulfonamides. The powers that be aren't worried about the way penicillin is developing, and anyway, sulfonamides are showing promise in diabetes. It's hilarious! The story goes that someone in England said about sulfas: "Piss on them!", so someone did – they mixed sulfa and urea, and, 'presto!', a drop in blood sugar. Who would have thought? What a wonderful business!" Darius replied, "It is a wonderful business, and I'll try to make it better. Have fun in Canada!" He laughed, hanging up.

"What an idiot!" They both thought.

Petr Chetkovsky and his fellow fugitive were able to make it to Warsaw without stopping for petrol or food. In spite of the stress, effort, and danger, they also arrived happy and contented. Regardless of being very seriously interrupted by the 'brown shirts', Fran, typically female, recalled hearing him say 'I love you', and reminding him, they spent most of the travel time resuming that conversation, and exchanging vows and wonderment, and the rest of the trip on plans for the future, both immediate and long term. Yes, Petr and his Fran were in love.

(This is the time when the re-teller of the story should describe all the wonderful feelings they have had for many years, but the restraints of time and space would make a second book probable. Ed.)

They would be married immediately in a civil marriage for two reasons: His priest or her rabbi would require too much preparation time, even if they could return to Krakow for the ceremony; and, a civil wedding would provide them with papers which would belie the fact that she is Jewish. If that was not sufficient for their escape, they would try to find fake papers, or change their names, or something!? The main hope was that this Nazi situation would soon be over, everything would return to normal, and they would then have a nice, big, proper wedding. Meanwhile, he would make do by giving her the small, almost feminine, ring he received with the chemistry medal; after all, it's all he had.

Their immediate need was rest, food, and shelter, and they had no luggage and little money until the banks opened tomorrow. "Perhaps some day banks will adopt sensible hours for customers, no their profit and comfort."

Petr decided to try to locate a friend from the days at university who had moved to Warsaw and taken employment at an analysis laboratory in a large hospital. They had an hour before closing time to find the hospital and find him. After finding out his address from the hospital payroll clerk, he knocked at his door.

"Hello, Herman, do you remember me?" Petr Chykovski asked. "Of course, how are you? Have you moved to Warsaw? And who is this beautiful lady?" asked Herman, his classmate for two years.

"Herman Chepoldy, this is my fiancé, Fran Dultz; we ran away to be married. We are "eloping"." While Herman kissed her hand and shook his, Petr explained, "We decided to come to Warsaw on a 'spur of the moment', but when we arrived, the banks were closed, and we must find a place to stay tonight."

"But of course, you can stay with me at my apartment, just like old times." Then, with a frown, he said, "But I have only one bedroom,...you could probably use the large chesterfield." Then, with a big smile, "This is wonderful! We will celebrate. It's time to close up here, just give me a few minutes."

Herman closed up, thinking "Why are they doing this so suddenly? There is more to this than meets the eye. I must watch closely for subterfuge as a good Nazi. They are suspicious! Maybe they couldn't manage a hotel without money, but why are they coming to Warsaw, anyway?"

Petr wondered if he could trust his old friend. Surely he wouldn't do anything to do harm to his old college buddy, I wouldn't do anything, surely he has his thoughts on straight. "Don't worry," He thought, "This war has us all crazy, it will be all right."

One of the biggest, unrecognised, problems of the war was the ability of people to believe that humans, being graduates of the "survival of the fittest" concept, should acknowledge beliefs of current religion instead of realising that we are just a higher development of the animal kingdom, and theories of "survival of the fittest" applies to us everyday, regardless of our wishes, or /and thoughts of theoretical enlightenment. To stay on top of the list of "best animal", we must consider what we are, and try to improve.

"

The café was small but appeared to be clean, and the food was good and not expensive. The three university graduates had lots to talk about and found many reasons to celebrate with the good wine served, including the invitation to Herman, that he be "best man" at the wedding tomorrow. They drank to another event, but not in celebration: Yesterday, the German army crossed the Polish border, and today many countries were declaring war. "Not a good start to the month of September. This month is usually registration month for the university term, filled with hope and optimism, and a whole new batch of freshmen and pretty freshettes. Instead, we have a new batch of Nazi invaders, here to help us solve the jewish question." With glass held high, Herman was proud of his little speech and did not notice the exchange of glances, or the palm-down wave his old friend gave his upset fiancé. Fran nodded in agreement, however, resolving not to react to anything that may be said. She raised her glass and dazzled them both with a radiant smile that lit up her blonde hair and deep blue eyes, "To peace soon, when everyone comes to their senses!" "Hear, here." all replied, and off they went to the apartment.

They were in a very relaxed state by the time they arrived at Herman's apartment, a very small two room unit at the rear of the third floor. He admitted to being "a bit tipsy", a new expression gleaned from an American movie, which sounded humorous in Polish. "Here we are, it's not much, but it is home to me. All the good jobs and the good apartments have been grabbed by the Jews, so this is all that's available. That may change soon," he said darkly, Then, with a smile and an expansive gesture, he continued, "Let's pretend tomorrow is today and you are married. You both take the bedroom and I'll sleep on this chesterfield. It was imported from England by my grandmother and is very comfortable for sleeping." To prove it, he stretched out, and was asleep in a few minutes, snoring as loudly as a great deal of wine induces.

In the bedroom, however, sleep came with difficulty. Both were excited and overtired from the day's events, and they also had a lot to talk about, mainly their deep feelings for each other and their unstable plans for the future. Petr was reviewing to her the many beauties of this fabulous creature before him, as she was telling of her love for him.

"I am the luckiest man in the world," he thought, "to even be considered for a relationship with this perfect, beautiful lady, much less to agree to be my wife. Her social standing is 'way above mine, and her beauty is so deep, so refined. She has that wonderful type of personality which announces angelic purity to the world, and, to complement that, her pale, smooth, clean complexion almost glows, and it is all framed by her shiny blonde hair. Probably even angels don't have eyes as deep blue, that sparkle when she laughs, with her eyebrows rising prettily. God! I love that woman."

In spite of the rising glow of need in his loins, he said to her, "You take the bed, and I'll roll up in that rug. I have too much respect for you and for marriage, and we are not really married until tomorrow. "You're passing up a sure thing.", she said, teasingly with a grin; then seriously, "but you're right." Alone with her thoughts, she was a bit disappointed, not only because she was feeling some desire, but she had also decided to try to start a family with this man tonight, and she was unable to shake a feeling of foreboding for the future. Her life, that of her family, and that of the whole world, seemed to be sinking into a long- lasting turmoil, in spite of everyone's hope that "this will soon blow over."

Petr awoke to the sound of murmured talking in the next room. Half awake, he began to analyse what had awakened him. It had not been loud noise, quite the opposite, and perhaps the quiet, covert sounds were so unusual as to be alarming. "Alarming is the word," he thought, now fully awake, "Fran is O.K., sleeping beautifully, and it must be early morning judging from the brighter darkness at the window."

He began to make out the words his friend was murmuring into the telephone, "…I know she is a Jew. I found that out back in university when I wanted to meet her. Perhaps they both are….?"

Herman was standing facing the telephone on the wall with his back to him, and did not see Petr swing the vase at the head of his (ex-) friend. He stood over him in amazement as the traitor crumpled unconscious to the floor. "What did I do? Did I hit him too hard? What's the matter with me; I don't do those things; did I really hit him?" He picked up the dangling phone, but the line was dead, and said to no one in particular, "That could have been anyone, maybe even the police. We had better run."

"What's wrong?" Fran asked, standing drowsily in the doorway, wrapped in bedding. Petr looked at her blankly, still in amazement, and thought, "how beautiful and vulnerable she looks. She is lovely – I love her – I could kill for her – perhaps I did!"

Aloud, he said, "He was reporting about us on the phone. Who would he call this time of the morning? We must go now, get ready." He ordered in a worried voice.

"I still can't believe I did that." Petr said to Fran while driving through the streets of Warsaw in the early morning. "I don't remember anything after realising my friend was giving us up. I became angry at him, and at the whole world, but I don't do things like that! I thought the vase was made of china, not iron." "His pulse was strong, I checked," Fran said, "he'll be all right."

As they rounded the next corner, they suddenly came upon a barricade. "Halt," said the guard, a soldier with a rifle. "Vas is los?"

"We are looking for city hall," Petr said, "we came to Warsaw to be married," offering his identification papers, "is it near by?" "It iss not dis way," the guard said in a thick German accent, "dis part off der city iss sectioned off for the protection off da juden." "Go back that way," he nodded, "you can turn here." Smiling at Fran, he leered, "I can see why you are in a hurry to marry her.", and he waved them off.

"Whew! At least we have found where your parents are." Petr commented, "I wonder how big a section is under guard?" Fran replied, "The signs are all pointing the other way, and there seems to be a fence past an open space. They are more interested in keeping people in, than out. After we are married, we may be able to drive right in." she realized.

After finding the marriage license bureau and inquiring about a license, they found that its formal cost was more than they had in their pockets, and they would have to wait an hour for the bank to open. They decided as well, that they should be prepared to bribe the clerk, who apparently knew how to make a strong, but subtle hint. The waiting line up was about three days long, but he suggested a way of shortening it.

By the time they found their bank, it had already opened, and a line up of several customers per teller had formed. They settled in to wait their turn nervously, but no one appeared to have any interest in them, although a few men tried to take surreptitious glances at her. "I must suggest to Fran that she disguise herself." He thought, "She is much too attractive, and she doesn't realise it."

Finally, the bank manager condescended to meet them, as is required by the new president for people they recognise as new, or potential, customers. "Your papers are in order, Mr. Chetkovski, but your account book could be more up to date. I will approve your draft, but if you are moving to Warsaw, perhaps you would prefer to transfer your account to us from our friends in Krakow?" he asked with a forced smile. "I will do that as soon as we are settled in, sir. We will know in a few days when the move is permanent. Thank you." replied Petr. The manager then took the draft to a teller who was finishing up, putting Petr at the head of a line, and said, with a fraction of a bow, "...welcome to Warsaw, sir.", and retreated to his office.

Fran had slowly moved toward the doorway, and smiled, and turned toward Petr at his touch on her shoulder. Her smile froze when she turned face to face to the bank guard near the open door, who was drawing his gun. Petr was still taking his cash from the teller, unaware of Fran's problem. "Are you a Jew?" the guard asked in a quiet voice, as Fran proceeded more quickly through the doorway. "No", she said quickly, and then realized that was a mistake, because he then said, "Show me your papers," and "halt!" when she continued walking away from the bank. "Are you a policeman?" she retorted, as they turned the corner. His answer was full of doom, "No, but they are," waving his gun toward two policemen coming toward them. "You were identified." he said, nodding toward the direction of the bank.

She looked, but of course they were out of sight of the bank, and there was still no sign of Petr. Panicking, she thought quickly, "If I call 'rape' he may have a good excuse to shoot me, and if I try to wait for Petr there may be trouble for him; I will walk towards the policemen, it is safer, and maybe they are coming for someone else and I can bluff. When that appeared not to be the case, she thought, "He should have hit Herman harder! At least, they will probably take me into that Jewish neighbourhood."

"How can I get a message to Petr?"

Her despair was complete when a huge, black police car pulled up beside them and she was hustled in.

Petr was in a state of panic. Where was she? It was as if she had vanished into thin air! She had been walking slowly out of the bank while he was finishing up and counting the money, but when he looked again – she was gone! He asked several people, "Did you see a blonde girl out here?" One man answered, "No, I just got here." Fear welled up in his body, followed by dread. He rushed in a big circle on both sides of the street, looking around corners and in alleys. No Fran!

Petr dashed to his car and tried to do a methodical search of the entire area, with no result. "Maybe she had an accident," he thought, "I will check all the nearby hospitals, but I had better be careful about asking the police. Perhaps if I reported witnessing a possible rape or an abduction, ….." he mused, "oh, god, I hope that's not what happened. I need some help, though, I will have to risk the police with some kind of story." Then, with a pang of real pain under his heart, he realised that he had her papers! He had offered them both to the clerk at city hall, and unwittingly, had pocketed them when he went in pursuit of money. Now she is in worse trouble; although she might be mistaken for a non-Jew, but without papers. He then stopped, closed his eyes, took a deep breath, and made a very sincere, one-on-one, complete, earnest prayer directly to his maker for her safe return; including admitting that he was way overdue in that activity.

Her picture on the identification card was unusual for a photo of this type, her beauty shone through the stark, unsmiling pose. Anyone who saw her would recognise her from this card, but it also described her as clearly being a Jew. "I can't use this. I had better hide it, for now." he decided.

Hours went by, and he continued to search the area over and over. His mind went over every possible scenario, and none were good.

He tried every idea he could think of, taking risks with a policeman on the corner, the bank manager, who was non-committal, but appeared to be unaware of any unusual situation, some other tellers, even the man he had asked earlier, still saw nothing-with thinning patience. That evening he took a small hotel nearby, and continued searching until it was hopeless. He then telephoned Basle, and left a message for Mr. Kunz.

Days went by, with nothing.

He was living a nightmare, where did she go? Was she taken or is she just hiding? I tried to be visible as much as possible so she could find me if she was able. She must have been taken, if she had an accident or heart attack……no, my imagination is running away…..she must have been captured. Is she being questioned? Tortured? Raped? Oh, God, please protect her, she is my life. Take me instead! Make it a trade if you have to. Take me anyway, if she must die. I must find her!

Finally, Petr decided he must enter what people were now calling the Jewish Ghetto. If she is still alive, she would go there to her parents, he concluded.

Meanwhile, Rick Carter was just hanging around. Actually, he was in his parachute hanging from a large branch about 40-50 ft. from the ground, and he had to keep quiet as three German soldiers were taking a break below him, at the base of his tree. He waited as long as he dared, they were lounging at the base showing no intention of leaving, so, holding his machine gun firmly, he hit the release device on his parachute and dropped beside them. He was shooting as he landed standing up and two of the three died instantly, and the third had his gun shooting wildly as he was hit and fell. The pain was almost unbearable when he landed standing up, and he almost fainted but fear overcame that, luckily. He soon realized though that something was wrong with both legs, waves of pain was coming from both as if they were broken, and he was unable to stand. Crawling quickly, he looked around, but no one was available to hear the noise, and, checking the soldiers, determined that they were all dead.

Sitting and catching his breath, Rick wondered how he could survive with two broken legs in an enemy's country, or at least, a country captured and controlled by Germans. He did not know the language except for several long curse words he and his pals used when he was a kid. He 'acquired' a jacket from the dead soldiers, torn a bit by bullets, but usable, and Rick mused at how the machine gun made so much damage. He quickly buried the unfortunate soldiers in shallow graves, and ran – hobbled -as far as he could from the scene. He slept in a ditch when the sun died and it was welcome, but fitful with the pain. Finally, he took a morphine tablet from his pack, and saying a long cuss word in German, fell asleep, not realising that a couple of teenage girls heard him. He was awakened in the morning by one of the girls with some bread and hot soup, and all he could do was say, "danka" and a long cuss word. So he smiled and shook his head crazily, and the girl retreated to her home. So much for his worries, he would act as a crazed army retiree, as he fashioned an old tree branch as a crutch.

4

WARSAW GHETTO: Absolute Hell

Surrounded by two fences or walls of barbed wire, old wooden fences, rubble, or burned out buildings, separated by empty spaces covered by checkpoints and machine gun posts –the guns pointing inward-, manned by German army guards, this "gated" neighbourhood for the "protection of Jews in Poland", was a huge prison, pure and simple.

Petr decided a before-dawn sortie through the most sound-looking burnt out or abandoned building forming part of the wall, would be safest and easiest, in spite of being out of curfew. If caught, he would tell the truth and trust to his papers to keep him alive, and if not, well, his life was not much good without her, anyway.

He chose the western side of the enclave in the hope that this side would be less closely watched for people entering, as German soldiers proliferated here. The side best guarded to keep people in, may be weakest in keeping people out. 'There is a chemistry principle in there somewhere,' he considered in amusement.

Big rats frequented this building. He wondered if the Germans had trained them as guard dogs, they were so large. Just a weak effort at humour, he commented to himself. The small, intermittent beam of flashlight peeking through his fingers did nothing to deter them, but it did prevent him from falling through a huge hole in the middle of the floor. The door at the other side of the building was not blocked as the front one had been, so things were getting easier.

Cold metal suddenly came against his throat, and "achtung!" was hissed loudly in his ear. He froze, while the man behind him said, "spieken zie deutsch?" In a panic, Petr could not think of one German word to say, and, still unthinking, blurted, "Please, I'm from Krakow", in Polish, and closed his eyes tightly, expecting the death blow. Instead, the knife relaxed slightly, and the man hissed in Polish, "Quiet!", then, "move", pressing him firmly toward the opening. Petr almost gagged at the big man's breath of onions, garlic, and kielbossa, but which created some assurance that the assailant was not German. Come to think of it, why was he using a knife, and not a gun? Perhaps it is robbery, Petr thought hopefully. "Do you want money?" he asked in a whisper. "Be quiet, or else!" the assailant muttered, "turn right, here". A car was waiting at the end of the street, with a driver barely visible in the pre-dawn light. "Get in." and they drove off.

In the basement of another abandoned building a short drive away, Petr realised that their interest was in questioning him, not robbery, and maybe not even murder. He eventually came to realize that not being able to speak German fluently probably saved his life. His reaction at the time gave them pause, and some small doubt that he was one of the spies entering the ghetto to select and identify criminals, Jews, spies, or others, more urgently wanted by the police or the Nazis. They had killed three already, they said proudly.

What seemed like hours of questioning and cross-questioning went by until he was so exhausted he was beginning to babble, but his story did not, of course could not, change. Finally, they gave him back his papers, holding back his auto registration, and quietly offered him a piece of stale, greasy, bread and some water. It was a banquet for him, and it, along with the more relaxed attitude, created a wave of emotion up to his throat and some tears in his eyes. "We have decided not to kill you, but we will wait until your story checks out. You will stay here for now, and we will hide your car that you left at the entrance – keep it safe. I am forming a plan which might help you find your fiancé, but we will need your assistance in return." He said, evenly and coldly.

"Thank you very much," Petr said sincerely, "I don't really want to leave here until I find her, and I will help any way I can. You know my car?"

"We have been watching you since you left it. We will hide it." Another man said.

Petr slept where he sat, and when he was shaken awake by his guard, night had fallen.

"Whew, I'm getting too old for this," he thought. "Keep quiet," said the guard in a whisper, "we are not supposed to be here. You must stay here, but not be found. They are shooting anyone they see out after curfew. They want all of us dead, one way or another. If they do find you, try to get them to see your papers before they shoot. You are a Polish citizen, not a Jew, and your papers are in order. Tell them you got lost, and found this empty building. Stay put, and good luck."

"Are you going to leave me?" Petr asked. "Yes, and don't try to follow me. Someone will come for you in the morning; he will tell you if your story checks out; and he is trying to get a message sent to Switzerland for you." The man said, buckling on another gun and holster, and continued, "Be careful, this "neighbourhood" is more like a large prison, and getting worse every day. You will find it harder to get out than getting in. So, good luck in your search, you're going to need it: there are over a quarter million people here, and more are coming every day, more than the Germans can kill. Goodbye."

Later, after he had disappeared, and as if to underscore what he had said, someone shouted in the distance and then machine guns rattled briefly. "I hope that wasn't him", Petr prayed.

Early the next morning, the guard he had first met returned to tell him his story checked out, and he had placed a short phone call to Basle and talked to a Mr. Grolimond. "He confirmed you, and that you are in great danger. He called this whole Jewish neighbourhood a death camp, which he called a 'ghetto' and a 'huge prison'. Also, there are rumours that this ghetto might be moved to a southern suburb, and that Himmler likes the plan because more Jews would die as a result of the move, and they could build a better fence or wall to hold them before putting them in it."

With a sad, stark, look in his eye, he continued, "I belong to a group of younger Jewish men who know that Hitler's final plan includes us. We fought a good battle weeks ago, but they were too much. We know there is little time for us left, so we are taking as many Nazis as we can with us. If you survive this, please tell the world what you have seen."

He proffered a piece of paper with two addresses written on it. "These two cafes are near the west side of our area, but outside," he said, "Your friend will be at one or the other at noon every day for as long as he can."

"Now, I have a job for you in return. The Germans, with the help of our own police (his look described his dark opinion of that), are trying to starve us or eradicate us any way they can, but they are allowing some medical supplies in for propaganda value. Some Americans and other neutrals, including the company we called for you, are donating it, but we have to bring them in. With your papers as a Polish citizen, you could use your automobile and bring them in without a lot of questions. The first shipment will have a million doses of a new sulfa drug from your company, called sulfasoxizole, supposedly better and safer than others."

Petr replied, "Yes, however, that is not my company, I just did some lab work for them. Can I continue to look for my fiancé?"

"Of course, but cautiously, and we are trying to find her for you also. There is one report that an old couple with that name was boarded onto a rail car with others, but we're not sure. They were alone. Usually, they don't take older people in the trains, as they expect them to die more cheaply here."

Petr mused to himself, "We have truly escaped into hell."

The resistance fighter continued, "You see, we are not very well organised here yet. No one is keeping track of people here, and the assumption is that they are all Jews, even though some are good Polish citizens, but are Jehovah's Witnesses, an outlawed religious sect. They must wear a purple star instead of a yellow one. We will get you a red cross on white armband and a flag for your auto. So, you need a good reason to be in here, and medical supplies transport fits well and works with a car. Can you add anything to your description of your fiancé?"

The word fiancé reminded him of her ring. She would stubbornly wear it, regardless of the risk, and never sell it, although maybe it has little value anyway, he thought. "Yes, I remember her engagement ring is all I had at the time. It has the crest of the Jagellian University Medical College, and the word 'CHEMISTRY' engraved under it. She will be wearing it on her left hand."

"I hope she's all right," the resistance fighter said, "anyone wearing a ring in here runs the risk of having their hand cut off, or more. This is not a nice place for wearing jewellery."

"As for you, we will get you out under cover of darkness tonight. My friend here will help you, and show you how to get to your auto. Rest and sleep now, we'll be back."

Suddenly, with this turn of events, Petr's spirits were improved, as things had taken a turn for the better. Now, he has friends helping him find his woman, they are looking for her ring, "I hope she still has it", he interjected; and he has an opportunity to come in and out of this virtual prison, even though it is still dangerous, but "I don't care" he thought out loud, "At one time, in the good times, I couldn't imagine a situation where I would really want to die, but if I were to lose her forever, forever would be too bleak for me, and I will gladly leave this world. Also, if I die trying to find her, it will be a life well spent."

Meanwhile, he mused, I can help with a voluntary program by Roche to reduce infection and pain for these helpless victims of madmen. I hope the world learns of this someday: the terrible, inhuman suffering an entire race is undergoing; and the way one research pharmaceutical manufacturer is able to help it. Humanitarianism should not be needed if there is no racism, but unfortunately there is.

As he settled down to sleep, he was not able to relax. The day had been very exciting, even scary. However, he continued to explore that train of thought as he tried to sleep, but excitement about the unusual activity he was to begin kept him thinking; but not sleeping. He continued to expand his thoughts about what he knew of this family owned private company in Switzerland, and how great was its contribution to medicine and medical research.

Also, he believed, knowledge of this pure altruism by a leading member of the worldwide pharmaceutical manufacturing industry may avert a worrying trend now starting: Some of the more inept physicians in many countries, including the United States, which had a legal structure based on suing for large sums and winning in spite of justice, started blaming their mistakes and/or ignorance on pharmaceutical manufacturers. They seemed to forget the concept that all drugs are poisons, and that they were supposed to know how to use them correctly. They, physicians sworn to "do no harm", were responsible for the correct use of the drugs they prescribe, and no one else. There should be no way that a physician can blame pharmaceutical manufacturers for the improper use, or negative outcome of any tool incorrectly used by them. That was their sworn duty, (and still is), Petr believed. A propaganda war was starting between medicine and pharmacy (manufacturers) which would be bigger than the propaganda war started by Himmler, Goebbels, et al., in this war.

Meanwhile, he could assist with the delivery of free medication such as meperidine (Demerol), sulfisoxizole (Gantrisin), total opium alkaloids (Pantopon), and maybe even Roche's multivitamin discovery; actually, they were all Roche discoveries. Petr continued to think of the wondrous project before him, and of the unfortunate amount of ignorance the public all over the world had about the current international pharmaceutical industry. This ignorance is even today fostered by the industry itself, he observed, as it is too complicated to understand by Mr. Average Man, of Anywhere, in this World, and so all of it is kept secret.

Still awake, Petr's thoughts and observations continued to drift:

"There are at least two main elements which are huge factors in this business: Patent Protection and Price, They are interchanged and connected; but not as the public perceives it."

"Take meperidine, for instance, simply a better, safer, controllable, drug for serious pain. Better than the world's leader: Roche's Pantopon (purified and standardised total opium alkaloids, 'process patented' for up to 50 years in some countries). Meperidine, marketed as 'Demerol', a patented Roche discovery, sold under license by Winthrop Laborotories in Canada, has become the most used new severe pain killer in the world, gaining its fame during this war. It is patented under older rules with longer protection, and its price is very low, often lower than Pantopon, which is much older."

"Most of the world doesn't know that price, now, has no relationship to cost. The cost difference to make 10 million meperidine tablets, instead of 9 million, is almost negligible. Manufacturing is only a small factor in pricing, protection of intellectual property is biggest. The manufacturer/developer must amortise over the period of protection, all costs of research, development (including my rewards), marketing, and then manufacturing, to break even or make a profit (which is their business model). If patent protection is poor, non-existent, or short, for instance, when some countries require only 5 years from discovery and 4 years is spent on required clinical tests and trials, you have one year only of marketing to amortise all costs just to break even. Switzerland is different, but it is a small country, protection there is just and fair, and that is why a big industry is allowed to flourish for the betterment of all humanity. Not only do some countries do little research on their own, but they don't offer much patent protection, either. However, the public blames the drug industry, not the politicians, for high prices."

(Author's note: While telling his story in 1966, Petr observed, in addition:

"If all the governments of the world offered reasonable patent protection, the world could afford free drug distribution funded by taxes. Yes, even the poorest country could afford free drugs as part of free medical care as a citizen right. The horrendous, unnecessary prices of medical care in the U.S., for instance, would be lowered with the destruction of health insurance companies. This would also destroy the "grifter" generic manufacturers making huge profits on someone else's invention. The answer is, full protection of intellectual property.")

This is why Roche was able to supply millions of doses free to the Warsaw Ghetto. For now, though, it's time to stop dreaming and return to reality. Some day the world will be in a better place, or cease to exist." Petr said to himself, turning over to drift into sleep.

The next morning Petr began his new job with a good feeling of optimism and renewed purpose. It was one of those clear, sunny days of relative calm and even a bit of warmth, rare in mid-winter in Warsaw. Driving toward the western entrance of the "Jewish neighbourhood" in his car stuffed with medications, bandages, blankets, etc., and festooned with white flags and red crosses, he began to hum passages of the new "Warsaw Concerto" only because he liked the melodies, and not because he was in Warsaw, and certainly not because his name was similar to that of the composer, as any connection to culture was frowned upon at present.

The gate was open, but no one was there to stop him, even greet him, he thought, ruefully. Nevertheless, he came to a full stop and waited for a while with his motor idling. After waiting for a polite period, and remembering that the guards were keeping people in and not necessarily out, he decided to move slowly ahead. At first he didn't notice the two men coming from a nearby doorway, one a civilian with a Jewish armband, and a soldier buttoning his pants. They were laughing, and in turn did not notice the ragged eight to nine year old girl following stiffly behind them.

She quickly came up behind them and opened her hands into an eagle claw position with pathetic nails exposed. She jumped onto the shoulders of the soldier in a valiant effort to claw out his eyes, screaming, "Momma's dead! Momma's dead. You killed her!" The civilian collaborator pulled her off the shocked soldier and held her by the elbows from behind. She still screamed, "You killed her! You....", which dissolved into a bloody gurgle as the butt of the soldier's rifle seemed to go right through her face, demolishing it. To make sure, he hit the face again and, sure enough, the butt went straight through probably to the spinal cord. She went limp, jerked with one small seizure, then lay still.

"That's one less Jew." the soldier said, still shocked, but relaxing. The civilian then said,

"She wasn't wearing an arm band, and she attacked you."

Petr, entranced and horrified by the vision, forgot the car was in gear and was rolling slowly into the compound until, relaxing the clutch too quickly, it jerked a couple of times and stalled before he could ram the clutch pedal back in. By then he was on the wrong side of the road heading for the curb, but corrected it just as the soldier called,

"Halt!" and raised his bloody rifle as if to fire at the sky. Petr halted.

"Give me your papers!" the soldier demanded. "Did you see that?" the other asked boldly, and Petr answered blankly, "What?" He followed this lucky answer with a flash of brilliance he later thought bordered on genius, "Was it an auto accident?" he asked, nodding back toward the body sprawled in the street. They glanced at each other, then, the soldier said, "Proceed", motioning him to hurry away before he changed his mind.

Petr started the car, changed gears with only a minor grind, and sped away with relief. "I am truly in hell", he thought.

He decided to judge the rest of this, his first day, on the balance of it; after all, it's bound to be better, and he must focus on finding Fran.

He was met at the hospital by two men, probably doctors, wearing red crosses above their Jewish arm bands, and shown around a burned out building with an undamaged ground floor providing a huge ward with an extra high ceiling because the second floor was gone and the third acted as a roof of sorts. The administrator, a kindly older gentleman doing double duty, smiled, "Thank you so very much for bringing this. We will use it wisely and sparingly, although most of our patients are beyond help. I read about the new, safer, sulfonamide, but never expected to have it in here. Are you going to the other aid station?"

"Sure," Petr said, "I didn't know about it. Where…..?"

"It was set up on the east side after the fighting. It was apparent that Hitler intended to kill us here, one way or the other, so some chose to die fighting. The patients are younger, and many are surviving major wounds instead of starvation or disease. The bandages and dressings will be of better use there, and, of course, the sulfa. I will send one of my orderlies with you, if you would go there today." "Of course I will," Petr said, "I'm also looking for my fiancé, who was last seen in here." offering her photo. "She is very beautiful, is she a doctor?" asked the administrator/doctor, noting her white lab coat.

"No, she is a chemist, but if she is able she might be helping out in a hospital here."

Nodding in agreement, the doctor said, "Unfortunately, these are the only 'hospitals', and we have no laboratory facilities, although it would be wonderful if we did; perhaps we could get some of those supplies. We sure could use her, but I haven't seen her." he said, raising his eyebrows at his colleague in question. The other shook his head sadly, and said, "If your donor could spare some of their total opium alkaloid preparation, we could help most of our patients pass on in less pain. People don't realize how painful the final stages of starvation are!"

Petr was struck with an idea: "Let's make a list for me to take back out. The Americans are eager to send anything they can. Only food is verboten. But, you know, Roche is the world's largest manufacturer of vitamins, and discovered many of them. Perhaps we could also get preparations like Ovaltine allowed as a medicine. Maybe some blood and urine testing equipment and supplies would help me find her; I'm not leaving this place until I do."

"Wonderful!" the doctor said, "When you get to the aid station, a Doctor Julius Mentz will help you complete this list."

Returning to his car, Petr walked through the many rows of patients, all of whom were emaciated, and some looked like living corpses lying there quietly groaning, hoping to die soon. It seemed sad but true, the best that one could hope to do is help them die more comfortably. As he continued that task, he again was convinced that he was now an inhabitant of hell.

The next stop did not change his mind about hell. The doctor there was a big, hulking man with large hands, completely unlike the typical studious doctor of medicine. He was quite frazzled and obviously exhausted, and his eyes were as empty as any man who has been in hell too long and has lost all hope. At the top of his list was syringes and needles (and maybe a new sterilizer?), not only for the pressing need to inject pain killers, if he were ever to get some, but to inject air bubbles into the arteries of those he judged terminal and in severe pain. As it happened, a demonstration of this occurred while Petr was there. A patient had been shot in the lower abdomen, causing a lot of intestinal damage and pain, but he had been responding somewhat to sulfonamides, at least for the infection, until they ran out. He had been screaming almost continuously for two days and nights, developing a strange pattern of disturbing sounds which reminded Petr of the last days of his grandmother, whose varicose veins had ulcerated in the legs, and developed gangrene. To the end, she refused amputation and died a horrible death.

The big doctor, with tears in his eyes, came to the decision that nothing Petr had brought could rescue the man, one of the younger Jewish men who had decided to die fighting when it became apparent that Hitler would be successful in his method of extermination here: by starvation! Putting together the old, bent, unsterile needle to the syringe, the doctor said to no one in particular, "It won't matter to him that this is a used needle, but it does to me." Then, pushing the needle into the young man's carotid artery, he said, "Goodbye, my young hero, god bless you." Taking a nearby bottle of alcohol for sanitizing, he had a good swig, wiped his eyes, and turned to Petr. "Will you put a better quality of alcohol on your list? This sometimes makes me sick!"

Petr made no comment, but said, "You must be overwhelmed treating such a large number of patients." The doctor replied, "Yes, there are too many, but the majority know why they are here, and I don't, cannot, treat malnutrition or hunger, and that is the main cause of death, thanks to Hitler and his gang. I try to treat pain and infection, and do surgery if it is indicated, and if it is not, in some cases, I use narcotics to full advantage," he said bleakly, "and the meperidine in tablet form will be very useful. Do you know its LD50 –the lethal dose? That is not mentioned in the monograph." "No," Petr replied, "I am just the delivery man, but I will ask someone who knows."

The doctor looked thoughtful and sad, replied, "In that case, can you get me some more ampoules of Pantopon? Any non-Nazis I find with something terminal, that is, something terminal SOON, I will relieve the pain and make the end come faster." Then he was reminded, "Can you get me a larger quantity of alcohol for sterilization?" He asked, taking a swig.

"Sure," said Petr, "and they want to send something called a multivitamin for trial. It seems Roche, the developer and manufacturer of most of the world's synthetic vitamins, has found a way to combine the minimum daily requirement of several vitamins into one pill, and obviously these people need a double dose. There will be no need to keep extensive trial records except quantity, name, and date, which I can help with, but everyone needs it and it might help me turn up my fiancée – she will use her real name, I'm sure of it."

The doctor was excited with the offer, "Yes, that is very kind of your company, but it must be called a therapeutic trial for scurvy, and calcium intake, and mental illness, or I will be shot." He prophetized, and nevertheless, six months later, he was.

"Set it up with Helga out front, I can trust her. You never know who is watching."

Later, Helga set up a small chart for name, dose, started/stopped, mouth condition, bone effects, etc. "The trial lasted about half a year until the Nazis got wise, and then sent most of the trialists 'away'. The results were never published, nor were they expected to be. Maybe the five million doses did some good, but we'll never know." Petr reminisced later, while telling his story, "One good thing I found out later is the doctor, a

German national, was able to keep a couple of meperidine for himself for just before he was shot."

"I hope not all of the good people of this world will be exterminated before this war ends, or that would leave a world of Nazis, and the end of civilization." He opined.

Petr passed around his photo of Fran and obtained promises from all that they would watch for her. While leaving, he thought that if she had to stay here, with no chance of getting out, at least he would know how to help her finish it. The drive back gave him time to muse on how much he loved her, and how much he hoped she had escaped this hell somehow. It was a long drive, and it was hard to see through the tears.

Petr found a reason to return to the "Jewish neighbourhood" every day, often creating his own reasons, such as starting a new aid station to the south, manned by American volunteer doctors – operating with impunity, even thanks, as they helped with positive propaganda in their homeland- assuming it remained neutral. To avoid suspicion, he used a different entry point every time-leaving the way he entered. Nevertheless, some of the guards began to recognise him as a "regular," and began to tire of checking his pass. This allowed him to think about bringing in other items, messages, money, etc., but his primary focus was on finding Fran, therefore food- verboten on pain of death- was out. They would shoot him on the spot if he was transporting food, although he would pack a good lunch every time. He would be no good to Fran or anyone else if he were dead.

His idea about the laboratory equipment worked to a degree, but it did not produce Fran. Operations began in a room of the new southern aid station under the part time management of a volunteer bacteriologist related to the owner of a pharmacy, just over the river Wisla, who was trying to support the resistance covertly. The bacteriologist's major specialty was not chemistry of course, although with the basic training from years ago, she could do some very necessary tests. Petr made sure a wide-spread call went out for anyone with training as a chemist. After a fruitless two weeks, he convinced some people on the outside to offer a small salary to anyone in the enclave who could fill the position. Many applications were received, and a couple were even valid, but Fran was nowhere to be found.

After the "suicide", as announced by the Nazis, of Dr. Mentz, the enclave found itself with a nicely equipped lab with both a chemist for blood and urine analysis, and a bacteriologist over-equipped with microscopes and petrie dishes, but no doctor to prescribe or analyse the tests!

Petr began to lose hope of ever finding Fran, much less her parents, and after months of searching for her, and transporting medical supplies and "vitamins" ostensibly, and counterfeit German marks and ration cards covertly, he was becoming too well known for his own security, as well as the security of his operations. When he was told of one, and then two, men asking too many questions about him, he began to recruit other drivers and substitutes to cover his trail.

He began to understand the fallacy of a public assumption that some very brilliant people were directing, controlling, and planning the various resistance activities going on around him in this place: A very good rumour mill was working well, some collaborators were dying of various bizarre "accidents", distribution networks were becoming efficient and less starvation was apparent – although this was due in a large part by the tacit agreement of all the inhabitants of each building that they share their resources equally among themselves. This was mutually enforced and controlled voluntarily, and bespoke of a higher degree of civilisation and human progress among the Jews than any other human race, and especially compared to the animalistic Nazis. The proof was there for any true racist to see.

In fact, no one was running the show! All of the brilliant and successful techniques of smuggling, sabotage, and resistance to invader and collaborator were the result of "on the job" training. The conceivers and executors of unsuccessful endeavours were all dead!

One of the reasons for the rumoured impending move of this "Jewish neighbourhood" was the overall success of resistance to this 'final answer' of Hitler's. His ration goal of 180 calories per person per day was never reached so far, and mass starvation was often being averted, and many systems and programs within the enclave were flourishing. Rumour had it that an area south of the Wisla river in one of the suburbs, had been chosen as it had more natural barriers to prevent escape, and to put more pressure on the population to starve to death. This seemed to remain as the best plan for Hitler's "final solution". With all of this relative success, and no sign of Fran's fate, he began to consider giving up. She was truly gone, and he was still alive.

Driving back to his hiding place in central Warsaw, Petr was in a reflective mood. "It's funny how things work out. Here I am, now still living in hiding in the same place I was taken to after capture a year ago, when it was part of the first Warsaw Ghetto. Now it's in an area of relative peace, with no gunfire to be heard. He remembered the incessant killing, the smile on the child's face after the soldier shot it, as if he did her a favour, and the faceless girl at the gate, and the old husband and wife, locked in a final embrace with their heads bashed in, the pile of bodies stacked in a pile in a ditch by the river and its smell, and finally, as if to block out the other thousand horrible images, he visualised Fran's face, smiling at him with that amazing, open, beautiful, loving smile.

Stanislaus, his old friend the resistance fighter, was waiting for him when he entered his apartment. "I may have some news for you, but it's not good." He looked hard at Petr, took a deep breath, and continued, "We found some collaborators this morning. Caught them red-handed and killed most of them on the spot, but one of my men noticed a weird ring on the finger of one piece of shit. We 'persuaded' him to tell us how he got it, and he finally told us that he took it from a woman he was herding into a train car going to Treblinka. The good news is that he said she was thin, old, and ugly, so maybe it was not your Fran. Jews don't return from Treblinka. He is probably going to die of his wounds, or whatever, but we are saving him for you to talk to; you will have to come now, though."

When they arrived, Stanislaus handed him a long thin knife, which Petr at first refused.

"Take it, and just hold it near his face. He is beyond caring about anything, but he has a strange terror of the stiletto near his face. He might tell you something else."

The prisoner was a smallish man who appeared to be totally wrecked. His hair was still black, except for the red smears of patches where it used to be. One ear was badly cut, a large bleeding piece dangled oddly, but his eyes were bright and shiny black, 'like a frightened rat', Petr thought.

Petr forced a stern voice, "How did you get this ring?", and he thrust it in front of the rat eyes. The prisoner mumbled something, and two words seemed to come by way of a bubble of blood which released the sound when it broke. "What did you say?" "How did you get the ring?" he repeated, but this time he had the prisoner focus his beady black eyes on the knife. The eyes widened, then looked at him. The wide, black eyes had a look of pure evil and hatred in them, and more audibly, he said, "Juden bitch."

Petr's earlier visualisations came back, but they were all one mishmash of pictures of piled, stinking bodies, killed children, people in the last gasps of death by starvation, and in the middle his Fran smiling her glorious smile at him. This man was the personification of all the evil propaganda the Nazis had created and fostered, but nobody seemed to do anything to stop, much less reverse. The frustration built slowly but quickly in his soul forming a passion too large to stop.

A strange hand pushed the stiletto under the man's chin and up with obvious ease through the roof of his mouth or behind it, with seemingly little bone resistance, to the hilt. The evil eyes suddenly looked funny as they crossed crookedly and froze in a weird pose. Someone said revengefully, "bigoted piece of shit."

Petr looked around as if to ask, "Who killed him? I might have…." Looking down at the hand that had just dropped the knife, and realising that it was his own hand, Petr sat down hard, dazed.

Stanislaus, the resistance fighter, came over, put his hand on Petr's shoulder, looked him in the eyes, and said, "It's all right, he was dead anyway. This is your first, and it's hard!"

"It's also my last," said Petr, still in shock.

He looked again at the ring. It was from the Jagellian University, but ARTS shone brightly. Wrong ring! This gave Petr two conflicting emotions: disappointment that he hadn't found a sign of her, but also the renewed hope that he would someday have better news. Also, the pain of knowing that he just killed someone was reduced a bit.

Still shaken and demoralized about the day's events, and with a sinking feeling that Fran was either dead or transported somewhere terrible, Petr decided to make tomorrow his final run into, and out of, hell.

Petr woke late the next morning, as if his decision of the night before had relaxed him, causing him to sleep late and more soundly. In a dopey, semi-awake state, Petr looked out the window to a sunny blue sky and mused, "This is one of those mornings, that is so nice if you keep looking up. The sky is clear blue with the odd small wispy, or puffy, cloud as an accent. The trees in the background are green, those that have survived, and if you don't look too close at your surroundings, all is good."

In close focus, the devastation and stink when you open a window is horrible. The Warsaw Ghetto, as it has come to be called, is a preposterous slum of buildings rotting and falling apart, some already down from the odd disposed of bomb – not even a considered or alternate target in the many bombing runs the allies have made, especially from Russian planes, as they are not allowed to return to land with even one bomb, however defective, left over. Or maybe it is a weak attempt at mercy killing. At least, most Russians know what part of Warsaw not to purposely bomb.

"Most of the toll on the buildings is natural, they have had no maintenance whatever for up to ten years. There are not many inhabitants left either: the healthy ones were sent off to be eliminated like my Fran, and the rest were old or very young and had to deal with medieval sewage, no public health or sanitation, little medical care – save for the generosity of companies like Roche with the benchmark single sulfa, sulfasoxizole, and synthetic vitamins to prolong the agony of life for a doomed people."

"I wonder what history will remember for us? Will inadequate doctors blame their shortcomings on drug companies? Will patients turn on them for prolonging the agony of life? Perhaps big research companies like Roche won't always be hailed as saviours of the modern world? Looking around, there is not much left to save." Now depressed as usual, Petr shrugged and went to work.

5

ESCAPE TO THE BORDER: War is Hell

Nazi S.S. Oberlieutnant Heinrich Schlager was the only officer in this entire Krakow Intelligence Headquarters without his own office. At least he had a desk to work with, but it was placed at the side of the main entrance opposite to the sergeant's desk so that anyone entering as a newcomer, or with any kind of questionable identification, would be sent to him by the sergeant for questioning. His pride grated at the thought that he was just a glorified guard, so he relished his other duties as a member of the bureau assigned to investigate questionable identities. It had been over a year since he had been berated by General Heidrich himself for "losing" the chemist and his formula for the "Valor" drug. He had not been allowed to protest in any way the implications in the report on his ransacking the chemist's laboratory. It was not his fault that he did not capture the chemist – he had not been told to. Nor was it his fault that he did not get the formula for the drug- he brought all the paperwork he could find. He even brought the chemical, all fifteen kilos of it (although the report said ten kilos- "I wonder who got the rest of it?" he mused.) He had been demoted and given the most miserable desk job his boss could find. Every day he cursed his luck, his situation, his boss, even the chemist who had started all this trouble. "I could be at the front, doing all the great stuff, developing my career with the help of the war, instead of sitting at this miserable desk in the backwash." He picked up a new file, applying only a part of his mind to it.

It was a report on a medical supplies driver in the ghetto in Warsaw. An observer had questioned the real name of the driver as a person he knew with a different name. A driver in the ghetto who may not be using his right name? That is similar to half the population of what's left. This is an idiot job. And, this Frances Dultz was only a Jew in a ghetto for Jews. Who cares?

Being alone, he thought out loud, "this is just another typical menial case I have to put up with, just because…." He paused, then went back to the paper he had thrown away.

The driver's picture gave him a strange, sudden sense of deja-vu. He thought, "He looks like any other Jew: gray, unkempt hair with receding hair line, glasses, full gray moustache, about 40-50, small build; an intellectual who looks like Einstein – so what?

"It doesn't matter," but he paused thoughtfully, "but why do I feel I saw him before? He paused again, took another look at the picture and the accompanying notes, shrugged,

"He is a Jew in custody in a Jewish ghetto, where he belongs." Something continued to nag at him. "That image is of a person I know," Heinrich Schlager decided, "but I don't recognize his name." ….. "Hmmm. He doesn't look very threatening, but…"

Suddenly, a commotion began at the front door. A man was singing in a loud voice, and another said, "Halt! Don't go in there!" The singer stopped, paused, then said, "I must go to my office. Don't stop me!" Another said, "Come, my old friend, we must go home." "No!" he said, just as Lieutnant Schlager opened the door. Major Schwimmer, his superior, almost fell in, gathered himself, and raised his hand to no one in particular,

"Heil, Hitler", he announced. "I will be in my office the rest of this evening, and I wish to be alone!" The sergeant exchanged glances with the lieutenant and caught the major before he stumbled again. The major fought off the assistance, and, in a studied, straight backed gait, made his way to his office, slamming the door. "Wow, he has a snoot full," he said, making noises like a pig, "I have never seen him like this." "Me neither," Schlager said, "I thought he detested alcoholic beverages. He must be celebrating something very important."

"Well," the sergeant said, "It's time for my 8 o'clock rounds to check the guard and then I'm off for home." "Lucky devil," thought Heinrich, "he goes home to that plump, full figured wife of his, and I have to stay until twelve, or later if the major stays. But there is no one waiting anyway."

"Sometimes I wish that fool of a wife had not been caught with the colonel. She completely wrecked my very comfortable life," he thought, aloud, he said to himself, "why do other people cause me so much trouble?" With that in mind, he was only half surprised when the gunshot rang out in his boss's office. He almost smiled at the apparent premonition. "It's going to be a long night," he said to no one in particular.

The next day was a continuation of the night before. Heinrich was not pleased with the way things turned out. Sleepless and discomfited with all the investigations, he was about to explode with anger when he was reminded that it was left to him to clean up the mess in the office. The major had put the gun under his chin, and therefore the bullet had lifted the top of his skull off, and blood and grey matter were everywhere. "I will not put up with this!", he proclaimed, "I am an officer of the S. S.!" The military policeman who had suggested he clean it up, said quietly, "whoa, don't yell at me. I just told you we are finished with the scene. You can clean it up, or stick it somewhere dark and dainty if you prefer. I'm leaving now."....and he also left quietly.

Heinrich Schlager did not really care, but found out anyway, days later, that his boss had been caught and found out by his superiors that he had been skimming the spoils of war. It seems that he had been found out underreporting that which his men "confiscated" over the years leading up to the invasion and control of Poland. One of the items, they had later discovered, was of a chemical slated to be delivered directly to the Reichmarschal himself. The major had kept a large quantity for himself, but then could find no buyer for it.

As Schlager slowly heard of this, piece by piece, he began to process it until a shock went directly to his lower stomach, and he sank down to his knees. With realization, the feeling of fear enveloped his whole body. "Mein gott, I am the next to go!" he exclaimed, "That dammed chemist!...", as he scrabbled for the picture he had seen that fatal night. "I must find that man, or his woman, my life depends on it" As he put on his uniform jacket and got ready to go, he thought, "He is the cause of all my troubles. If it weren't for him, I would be a major now, maybe even a colonel. I would not have been wounded by that Jewish jackal in the revolt, General Heydich would not have nearly had me shot, and I would have been a heroic leader of the soldiers of the fatherland. I will volunteer at once to go back into the Warsaw ghetto, and I will find him, with or without that formula."

Darius Kunz decided that he could wait for Petr no longer, he must be taken safely to Switzerland, and maybe the United States for now, regardless of how the war was going. For months now, he had maintained a bi-monthly rendezvous with him, only to be told of a new lead or development each time in his search for his fiancé' which, he had long since guessed, was unrealistic and sometimes fictitious. Meanwhile, he had arranged for millions of drugs, vitamins, food supplements, and surgical supplies to be taken by Petr into the Warsaw Ghetto, and all this seemed to accomplish was frustration by Hitler and Heidrich that fewer Jews had died than was planned. "Thank God for such mercies," he considered, in one of his few religious moods.

"We must finish this now. Let others take over the deliveries. Forget the girl (mmn, she was nice though.)." He said out loud to no one. "There are others after him. I wonder if the American ever went to Treblinka? He will not be happy when he realizes I sent him on a wild goose chase. But, he's a killer, and I believe, his goal was to "catch him or kill him". Perhaps he is working for Pfizer or Lilly, and I don't intend to lose him to the American Pharmaceutical Industry. Now that my nemesis, the German officer that chased us through Krakow years ago, has shown up again, we have to go!" Darius realized he was reviewing arguments to present to Petr Chetovsky, while driving to his final rendezvous with him, "…and another thing," he thought, adding to his arsenal of excuses,

"I am getting so nervous that I'm having bad trouble sleeping at night, and I hope I'm not getting addicted to the new benzodiazepine nitrate."

With this, he started to muse about the incredible pharmacological properties of this chemical. "We have to figure a way to explain in a straightforward way to the medical professions the actions, and sometimes the opposite actions, of different salts, and even analogs (mirror images, etc.) of this chemical to present innocuously before and during marketing. No small challenge as there is very strict regulation in most countries, and also, doctors being "experts" in medicine, must be led to believe, rather than being told," he told himself, and musing further, "If you look at the spectrum of main effects of the chemical as it's salts and analogs of each chemical cousin, the oxides seem to have no CNS depressing, or a very specific one, but then going to the other end of the spectrum, the nitrates of each, there is very much CNS depression, or its much more generalized. So whereas one extreme, chlordiazepoxide, shows only very specific activity on the amygdala the nitrate, for example nitroxepam, shows very strong generalized effects, but in both cases tests on addiction potential and other side effects were minimal, and the safety on overdose was incredible. Except for the potentiation of alcohol in the nitrates was very high, unlike the oxides-in which hardly existed." Darius, always amazed at the marketing potential of this chemical family, muttered to himself, "It will make a good sleeping pill some day" and he had "obtained" a few pills for the rare time he couldn't sleep – but without alcohol, or one might go into a coma for days, or worse!

"Darius was right, Treblinka is just a small village with a nasty smell," Rick Carter decided, "It has a rail spur, and trains come in secret, but there is no evidence that anyone of any importance was brought there and lived to tell about it; I would dig deeper here, but I know that Swiss S.O.B. just sent me on a false errand. I will get back to Warsaw as fast as possible. What a curse to have broken both legs while parachuting into Poland. The resistance was good to me, but I lost so much time! Good thing I accomplished other things over here, especially the enigma thing. My papers showing me to be a wounded veteran and hero of the Third Reich have been the best thing, thanks to my childhood hobby of memorizing long German cuss words and acting like an idiot" Rick thought, as he decided to stay on the train going back.

Rick Carter, having left the train at the Warsaw central station, made his way as quickly as possible south to the meeting place Petr had told him of, in the southern suburb called Wisla. He had told Petr of a codeword that he hoped would clear him of any suspicion that this Roche representative would have about his intentions, if a Mr. Grolimond with Roche had passed on this information, as it would identify him as an agent for the

American military, which was now helping defeat the Nazis. Otherwise, there might be a shootout, because Dr. Chetovsky would be accompanying him back to Switzerland and then the U.S., or else! He touched his hidden pistol in its holster for reassurance. Luckily, he met Petr near the entrance to the café and they entered together.

Darius was at the café near the pharmacy on Praga Street early, as he had been every second Monday for months, and he was all ready to force Petr to come to Switzerland today. He even had his bags packed and had checked out of his hotel, and loaded his pistol if he needed to threaten, or even kidnap, him. This was it, and no argument! After a tense wait of perhaps ten minutes, Petr came walking into the café with the American in crutches, Rick Carter! "Uh, oh, here comes trouble," Darius mumbled to himself, "how did he get back so soon?"

"You sonofabitch! You knew Treblinka was a dead end! Were you ever given the codeword?" Rick said, fondling the loosened and ready gun for a quick draw. To Petr, he said, I am taking you to Switzerland now, no excuses, with or without his help!" "Whoa!" Petr yelled, and stepping between them, said, "perhaps you're both right. I had words with a collaborator who thought he had put my fiancé on a cattle train going that way."

Darius said, "I'm sorry, but I was told the codeword only recently. I didn't know you were military, you could've been the competition; what was it?"

After exchanging the correct password all around, they ordered a drink and relaxed. Rick told a little of the story of what he had been up to over the years since he had crashed while landing. While in the hospital, after being made a "Nazi hero", he was able to learn that a code machine named "enigma" had been left in a little village on the French coast called Dieppe, he reported it, and then learned that the American navy had landed a battalion of "crazy Canadians" in a suicide attack, maybe because they spoke the same 'old' French dialect, on the same village. Most were killed, and he didn't hear what happened to the machine. Strange things were happening in espionage ever since, though. For example, he found out about a German submarine parked under the radar cover of the main entrance buoy of Halifax harbour in Canada, where all the convoys gathered for Europe, but nothing was done about it, in spite of reporting it several times. A village near a city called Moncton, New Brunswick, in Canada, had its name changed to Dieppe.

Finally, after much discussion, it was agreed to risk taking the next train west which would eventually end at the Swiss border. Rick would assume his role as a German wounded veteran suffering from shock, and eventually become friendly on the train as a fellow passenger, while Petr would be his normal Polish national self with business in Switzerland with Darius, and under his passport and papers.

They hadn't considered Kapitan Schlager, who was catching the same train, and had followed them after spotting Petr in the entrance to the café, and was following all back to the station.

6

Serendipity?

On the train, still called the "Orient Express" by the locals, the three settled themselves. Rick, according to plan, chose the adjoining car, and Darius and Petr sat together, putting some baggage on the two seats facing, so they would be able to stretch out. They were reassured that this train was going south once in Germany, at least to the Swiss border, in spite of there being a war going on, according to the ticket agent.

The train made a sudden lurch, as it always does when starting, reminding Darius that he should take a bathroom break before he settles down to a long trip. Soon after he left, Petr was shocked when Kapitan Heinrich Schlager, an officer of the S.S., abruptly sat down in front of him pointing a gun. Two other soldiers stood in the aisle. "You are under arrest, Dr. Chetovsky, on many charges, including selling secrets to an enemy. I am taking you to General Heidrich himself. Sit down!" He said, as Petr automatically rose in surprise and indignity. Calling him a "doctor" also did not go unnoticed, although applying this to a chemist is a common move of respect and awe by the public, albeit inaccurate. At the time, he chose to leave it be.

As he returned, Darius was surprised to see this scenario, and he reached for his gun, but thought better of it when he noticed the two soldiers watching him. "Sit down!" Captain Schlager repeated to Darius, "as you are a Swiss national, I won't arrest you, but as a probable conspirator, I invite you to join us or you will be shot!" To the two soldiers, he ordered, pointing at them, "If he moves, kill him. If the other moves, wound him and hold him." "I will be right back."

Putting them under the watchful eyes of the soldiers, Schlager found the conductor and said, "Drop everything, you can take tickets later, I must send a message to General Heidrich at once!"

In the wireless compartment he dictated, "Send this utmost top priority to General Heidrich at the Nazi Headquarters in Berlin," so, the operator sent to the nearest Nazi headquarters in Warsaw to be sent further, top priority. Warsaw heeded the urgent and top priority request to Berlin, via the 'Enigma' system, reading: "I have captured the chemist, Dr. Chetovsky, who developed the 'drug of the valiant', and am now bringing him directly to you on the "Orient Express" train. Kapitan Heinrich Schlager, S.S." He returned to the 'doctor', handcuffed him to his wrist, and told all and no one in particular, to relax. Everyone did so, including those in the car who noticed the commotion but pretended not to. Later, when the train made its first stop of many, the soldiers were dismissed because of a growing shortage of personnel and because Schlager preferred to be in control alone. He would bring them in alone, without sharing the glory.

Rick Carter wondered why he was here; 'Here I am, a quiet, unassuming ex-pharmacist who never hurt anybody, in a foreign, war torn country with orders to kill, but with two broken legs- one healed well and one did not- leaving me with a limp at best. My saving grace was my ability to curse in German, learned from a friend when I was young who had a shoe repair shop. When I was a kid, I thought it fun and I did all my cussing in German. I certainly stood out in a crowd, some German cuss words take almost an hour to say."

"Unconscious and taken to a German hospital where I was babbling cuss words as I came to, it was assumed I was a German soldier with a memory problem hanging half dead from my parachute. That saved my life. When they asked why I was out of uniform, I cussed. When they asked how the legs felt, I cussed. Basically, I knew some German, but I knew a <u>lot</u> of German cuss words. After a while, everyone seemed to assume that I was some kind of crazed, cussing soldier, a wounded hero of the Third Reich. I milked it, but realized that I was in a precarious situation albeit with a good, unusual cover."

Rick continued to muse, "There are four men in this rail car associated to one situation and connected to the same event, but each is totally different in every way. This war does that, it makes strange associations.

Now, I must use that to somehow rescue the situation, but how?" He thought, as he watched the situation unfold before him.

Maybe it was a coincidence, but the next day the resistance fighters in Poland started to prepare an attack on the Orient Express near the Polish-German border, such as it was.

That night, Schlager tried to demonstrate to his prisoners how good he was as a guard, handcuffing them to their seats, accompanying them to the washroom, sleeping with "one eye open" to discourage them from taking advantage, informing each conductor publicly that they should be watched, as they are dangerous, and so on, so that their hope of escape started to diminish. After all, they were going "directly to hell's headquarters". After a few hours and a complicated dinner in the dining car, all, even Darius, began a fitful sleep, awakened occasionally by Schlager to demonstrate how lightly he slept and pointing out that thoughts of escape were out of the question. And so, the lurching, rolling, train chugged through the night.

Rick Carter was surreptitiously watching this and showed no interest in Schlager as they passed him on the way to and from the dining car, hiding his face behind a newspaper or his hat and keeping his crutches out of sight. Cursing his lack of mobility, all he could do was stay low and watch for an opportunity. The opportunity would have to be very unusual to have a chance to be successful, he thought, but on the other hand, maybe a simple, frontal attack would take the German down. Perhaps I will follow them back from the dining room this evening, take him out with a single shot, and try to get them off the train before night falls, and before we reach the German border with its usual train search. As the day went on, this plan seemed to grow as the best course to take, but for some reason he hesitated.

Heinrich Schlager started to relax a bit with his two prisoners, who, during this second day together, seemed to have a lower degree of resentment at being captured and cuffed. After all, the doctor would probably be put to work by General Heydich, the second most powerful German in the world, and it might be in a Roche laboratory in Switzerland where they already are miles ahead in developing his chemical. This was the general subject of conversation at dinner, which, by the time dessert was reached, they were almost friendly and some cooperative situations were explored, as Roche was held in quite high esteem by the medical community in Germany, Switzerland was being held quite unusually neutral by all the warring nations including Nazi Germany, and all three diners had more or less the same goal, to allow Dr. Chetovsky to continue developing his drug. Darius chipped in his example about a company in Copenhagen, Denmark, or was it Sweden?, that was actually being helped to develop a way to make penicillin more active when taken by mouth, instead of having to inject it, which is always more dangerous. Schlager ordered another bottle of wine to celebrate the more cooperative mood. Petr then suddenly changed the subject to sleep, mentioning how Darius would be able to sleep better this night over last. He held his gaze in Darius's eyes until the light of realization turned on.

Something that always fascinates me, and anyone really thinking about it, is the ability sometimes to project a thought wordlessly through the eyes. "I need one of your sleeping pills now!" Looked Petr to Darius. This wordless transaction was a great example of mind- reading, kharma, supporitive intuition, or whatever you call communication through the spoken eye. Kunz knew what Petr said, and meant, and he got an answer, without a word being said. Under the table a small pill arrived in Petr's hand, and he smiled quickly and briefly, a 'thank you' in return. All the while Heinrich Schlager was pontificating on the virtues of the Third Reich.

When Petr dropped the small pill into Schlager's drink, he wasn't bothered by any other question than, 'Will the chemistry be changed by the alcohol solution and maybe not work?' Such a concern could only be considered by a chemist! Dutifully, Schlager started to snore in five minutes, and lost a discernable pulse in fifteen, he wasn't dead, but almost. Hopefully, no one was going to check. What now? The two men practically carried Heinrich back to his seat in a couple of cars forward, without gaining much interest among other passengers who were used to Nazi officers having too much wine, and they were joined by a wounded veteran in crutches, who asked the same question again: "what now?" Rick was concerned about getting off the train quickly, as they were nearing the German border, which meant that the train would be searched and checked, and they would be found out. He was quite familiar with the terrain in this area as he had parachuted in and broken his legs here. They had just sat down and removed the cuffs after a long search for the key, when the train hit the bus.

A sudden deceleration as brakes were rapidly applied, the inertia was incredible- everything in the car flew forward, pummeling the passengers with a variety of shrapnel for seconds as the train tried to stop. Then a sudden bang and increased deceleration as it hit the bus, slowing it all faster- too fast, the second car behind the engine lifted slightly losing contact with the rails, it hung in the air then, in slow motion, fell, chewing up the tracks for another hundred feet as it slowly stopped, reluctantly. The rails had gotten so hot that they had started a small grass fire in the chewed-up sod. People were yelling and screaming, and some were starting to bleed as they picked themselves up, or started to groan or scream in agony. Everyone who could, started to leave at once. Pandemonium.

Schlager slept soundly through the whole thing. "I hope he's not dead." Petr thought, fingering a bruise on his cheek. "Everyone O.K.?" He asked. "Yes, but Carter's out, and bleeding!" answered Darius, actually, Darius had what turned out to be a dislocated shoulder, but used his good side, and, with Petr on the other, they carried Carter out of the teetering car and away to a small clearing. Everyone was milling around in confusion. A piece of broken crutch had stuck in Rick's side, and as he came to, he pulled it out, causing more blood to flow- not squirt, a good sign. With a bandage on it, and a painful but necessary manipulation of Darius's shoulder, all three passed muster, more or less. Petr thought about the engineer, who had been killed. He was a German national, but was just doing his job innocently, a casualty of Hitler's efforts.

Soon a man ran up to them and muttered the codeword, then said, "Follow me.", and as quickly, moved to a waiting auto. When everyone had barely piled in, the car sped away.

The driver, in poor Polish, told them what had happened. The bus driver had escaped the empty bus unharmed, as he had done before, and the target for the resistance group was actually the last car in the train which held a company of Nazi soldiers guarding a large collection of art and valuables destined for the Nazi headquarters in Berlin, with orders to redirect the train to an unusual stop there and unhook the car.

'That's how we found out about it." He said, noting that the railway was never happy when the "Orient Express" was used for illicit purposes. The Nazis had been "captured and neutralized" and the valuables put in safe storage. One of his group had recognized Petr from the Warsaw ghetto and his drug deliveries. He would not explain further, as the large car sped south roughly parallel to the German border. As the driver sped along, a Mr. Tzorac, a Czech freedom fighter, almost burned out but still alive, started to share his dream with whoever was listening as he drove. Some slept, some dreamed their own dreams, but Petr listened to every word, vicariously comparing it to his own- and Fran's – dream.

"When this war is over, and they always end, I am going to find Marie, only a pre-teen child when I met her a few months ago in Italy, but we bonded, and there is something about her. Anyway, I will marry her, if she will have me, and we will go to a new country where there is lots of room and opportunity, I have learned a lot about Canada from some soldier friends in a regiment called "North Novies" of the Canadian army in Italy and maybe I will find a town with a coal mine, like my hometown in Czekoslovakia where I worked before, maybe we could go there. Some of the Canadians were from Springhill, a mining town with a nice name."

Rick Carter chimed in: "I was in Canada for a while. It certainly has lots of room."

Petr smiled, if I had found Fran, maybe we could have gone there, too. "My God, I miss her. We could have gone to Canada, too." Thought this man who was near freedom. Now in relative safety, all relaxed and some slept. Petr reviewed the strange, often violent, life he had led for the past few years, such a difference from the plodding, humdrum life of a chemist, except for the occasional excitement of a realization or even a discovery. He did not like the way things were going in his current life. He had killed (albeit the man was dying anyway) the collaborator in Warsaw, and now he may have killed the German officer! Of course, he was another enemy of Poland, so I should feel better, but I don't. No matter how hard he squeezed his eyes shut, he could still see in his mind's eye the life leaving the eyes of the man as he pushed on the stiletto, the eyes went slightly crossed and the light slowly went out. He was also an enemy of Poland. Petr's eyes were now watering, maybe because they were so tight. "There is never enough reason to kill." He muttered to himself. Then he relaxed and thought, "Humans have been killing each other for millennia, giving themselves all kinds of excuses, but the basic reason is primal. Men, in order to in some way protect the entrance of the cave (looking without), and women, to protect within (i.e. the contents, the nest, the progeny inside), both have the same incentive: To protect preservation of the species."

The problems are the same: ignorance and imagination, two examples of the human state, creating fear for the nest, and/or the development of a perceived way of controlling others to the ultimate benefit of the nest (common to both genders). Imagination can alter ignorance, and ignorance fosters imagination. In the two millennia of Christianity, the current "good idea", those two factors have won over everything, and this war is proof of it. It may take something very strange to stop it, maybe what some are playing with, called nuclear fission. There is still never enough reason to kill, but we may make some progress yet. Mr. Nobel, a chemist and inventor of dynamite, is offering a very handsome prize as a reward for peace. Hope it works. (Author's note: A small coastal town here in Nova Scotia, called Pugwash, won a Nobel Peace Prize for hosting a 'thinkers' conference of leading world thinkers and inventors of atomic power, during the 'Cold War', the same time that Dr. Chetovsky told me his story.)

The trip was uneventful, the driver kept off the main thoroughfares between Munich and Salzberg, until they arrived in Lichenstein, where they used a passenger named Tzorac to drive, who knew the dialect as well as the language, for the guards, and was on his way to Switzerland as well. He was hoping to marry a young Italian girl he had met, and they would hope to emigrate to America, maybe Canada, if all went well. This appeased the guards, who let them pass through.

When Petr heard that, he had trouble swallowing his heart, and thought of his Fran.

They finally arrived in Basle, Switzerland, where the Swiss welcomed them with open arms. But Petr did not really relax, if ever he could again, until the plane landed in Argentia, Newfoundland, a British colony but in North America, a necessary fuelling stop, where he finally felt safe.

7

THE SEQUEL: Sobibor

Sequel? ....Ever hear of Sobibor?

One day in 1961, an old man approached the gates of the Hoffmann-La Roche compound at Nutley, New Jersey, and asked for Doctor Petr Chetovsky (his pronunciation). No one had asked this way for the Director of Research in a long time, in fact, the last sole visitor, an escaped psychotic Nazi officer, had been involved in something sinister and been shot to death at the entrance over ten years earlier. This sudden approach was passed on instantly to all the staff as if they had a super electronic means of communication such as exists decades later. Everything stiffened up, the guards suddenly got sharper and fondled their weapons thoughtfully, calls were sent, some even to Dr. Chetovsky, who considered this new visitor in the light of past events. Finally, he gave in to curiosity and asked that he be brought to him, under guard –as an after thought, but comfortably.

Colonel Nevid Koronski finally met Petr in his office after a thorough review of his credentials and a thorough check of his story by the guards, one even calling a contact in Washington. Petr was concerned about this apparent lack of hospitality, and apologized profusely, but the Colonel understood as he was a Russian visitor to a polish expatriate in the United States during the height of the "cold war". He explained that he had made a promise to a hero in WW2 and had traced Petr through records at the University of Krakow to this company and him by the prize ring he had been told of on the now missing finger of left hand of the hero who had saved his life.

All the emotion, love-hate-loss- suffering-and sadness welled up in Petr and almost swamped him. Is there never to be an end to this horror story? He could visualize his long lost lovely blond haired, blue eyed soul-mate being torn apart by jew-hating Nazis somewhere in a dark concentration camp like wild dogs, her fate unknown and unwept forever. Who was he to bring it all back? This better be good............!

Nevid had been captain of a company of Russian soldiers who had gone too far too quickly chasing the Germans out of Stalingrad. After many days fighting their way west and south giving retribution to the exhausted Nazi troops, their eagerness took them into a valley cut off from the rest of the Russian army and a trap by the Germans with a pincer movement from both sides. In a hopeless situation, their group consisting of tired old men –some as old as 60, all that was left to fight-, they had to surrender, and they were sent to the closest concentration camp, luckily, as it would have been more expensive in materials and men to execute them. They were sent to a camp in a town called Sobibor, near, but not Treblinka, Poland. This camp had been set up for prisoners which were more interesting than Jews, where the emphasis was not on extermination as much as keeping the inmates out of the way. They were on a shelf, so to speak. These prisoners were allowed to scrounge for, or grow, their own food and look after themselves instead of being starved as the cheapest way of extermination. They were 'good garbage', so to speak.

There this Russian soldier met the most fascinating, beautiful (once cleaned up and fed), intelligent woman he had ever met. He apologized for falling in love with her, but admitted not to have touched her, she was against that. They became friends, however, and she told him about being married to you, the love of her life, and told him of her wedding ring, cut off while she was unconscious and left for dead; the one you had won from the university in Krakow for making some chemical breakthrough. "That is how I traced you, "He said,

".....So that is how I came to know her. She was in frail health, as we all were, and she was sure that she would not survive this camp, even though she had survived Treblinka through a thread of good luck. She made me promise to tell the world of this horror if I survived, and to try to contact you if I could ever, to tell you that she loved you. (She was) an extraordinary woman."

"Yes." Said Petr, "I killed the man who cut her finger off to get the ring, he apparently was Russian, but a collaborator. You are the first I have ever told this to." After he deciphered Petr's poor Russian, he said, "He deserved to die for that. I would have killed him myself."

Petr reflected on how easily we discussed killing, as if it was a common activity. How strange the relationships were as a result of the war.

The colonel continued in broken English,

"Apparently, she had befriended a guard, a German officer who hated his job and eventually committed suicide, but who had her sent to Sobibor with the thought that it was safer. As it turns out, it was not. As the war went against Germany, the leaders of the Third Reich began to panic, and not all the decisions were wise. They decided to close the less important camps and somehow Sobibor got on the list, even though it contained many political prisoners, many German. Unwittingly, closing a camp meant killing all prisoners, regardless of political potential, especially as the front was getting closer, and even worse, they somehow let the prisoners know the closing target date."

"So, the safer concentration camp suddenly became a death trap with no options, and they even knew the date of execution! The prisoners, many of whom I befriended, looked to me and my men as the only hope because we were soldiers and knew how to fight. We were chosen to lead a suicide escape, whether we wanted to or not. We were tired and old!"

"Some situations lend themselves to heroism without any choice or planning. There was no deciding (Example: 'I guess I'll be a hero today!'), no choice of leader, no choice of who will go- we all go or die-, no planning necessary, except for the time. The time was discussed, when are the guards least likely to expect an escape? Even that train has left- they are on high alert. The only thing they didn't know is how fast we could make or acquire weapons, that was the only thing we, as soldiers, were extra good for. Otherwise, we must fight for our lives! We spent every minute preparing, training and discussing, making weapons, and preparing."

"They left it to me to choose the time, and we were to have no more than two hours notice, for security. That weight was heaviest on my shoulders. Many would die, maybe all! I chose the mid way between when we found out, and the announced date of closure as when the guards would be more relaxed and bored, I hoped. It made sense. I would announce the time when the situation seemed best."

"About two weeks into the month we had, many of the guards fell ill of dysentery. Maybe it was an act of God, or the act of those prisoners given the duty of sanitizing and cleaning the toilets, so I chose two hours after sunset, hoping the guards slept soundly. Those with knives were assigned the guards on duty, to cut their throats. The vanguard had a couple of rifles and a pistol, hidden for months. A hole was surreptitiously cut in the wire and covered, with prayers. The rest would be luck!"

"Some of the advantages unwittingly given to the prisoners were the lack of light given, so that most prisoners had better night vision than their captors, and the relaxed atmosphere historically given the 'political' prisoners allowed them to know their surroundings and geography better than most others. These advantages were well known to all prisoners, but the best advantage was that they had a leader, a military man they trusted to know something of strategy and opportunity. Some prisoners were even optimistic."

"At around ten o'clock, five throats were cut, but the sixth slept soundly as the woman with the knife couldn't bring herself to cut him, and later he shot her. The man assigned to shoot the guard in the tower missed, but got him on the second shot, then died of his wounds- he had been cut in half by the machine gun he was to take out. The second rifle succeeded in cutting down all that came out of the latrine. But the alarm had been sounded. That I know of, about half of the camp passed through the hole made in the wire. Another hole was to be made in another area, and a fire started near it, but I got no reports on what happened. I was hit in the shoulder about six inches from my heart, fainted momentarily, and woke up to your wife being a hero, dragging me to safety. Once in a depression in the ground, she rose slightly to stretch her back, but she was shot. I killed the guard but she was dying. She said, 'Tell the world about this, and tell Petr I love him.' I ran, I could not help her, couldn't even thank her, I was bleeding, and trying to stop it and hide at the same time."

Just a few years later, in the mid 1960's, as the waiters at the Waldorf started to clear the tables, Petr cleared his throat and said to me, "His story ended so abruptly that I thought I was in a trance. But he had nothing more to tell me. When he stood up, I shook his hand, thanked him, and he kissed me, then he said, 'I hope Russia and the United States become friends some day. Maybe Canada can help, it is right between us.'"

So Petr said to me, "Perhaps there is more to coincidence than we think,... you are from Canada. That is the end to my story, but I have no hope of getting it out. The company wants no publicity and will fire me or anyone who challenges that. I am old now, and weak, so no one will hear the story except from you. The world changes so fast, you might have a chance." With that, he mounted the podium to acknowledge his discovery of Valium (the drug of the valiant?). I was a 28 year old kid, trying to climb the slippery ladder of 'success',.... maybe when I retire." I decided, but I never forgot about it.

THE END

Contents

Prologue

Recap of Strange Associations to Nov., 1943

This is in the worst of the worst part of World War Two, in the worst part of Eastern Europe, at the worst time in the life of an escaped, wounded Nazi extermination camp survivor, therefore at one of the worst periods for a female escapee who is Jewish.

Hitler seems to be at his peak, all of Europe- including much of Eastern Europe- even a large part of Russia, is under his control. If Fran survives her wounds, how will she survive her position and will she have changed herself to survive? Will she have become sufficient enough of a survivor to become one?

Meanwhile, we can apply some conjecture to other thread ends left in "Strange Associations" as they apply to Fran, or both, when they were together such as: Did the Nazi captain get killed or did he pursue either one? What happened to the Judas friend, did he cross paths again? Would Roche make any attempt to find the other partner in the discovery of the benzodiazepines? If it was considered a 'secret weapon' early in the war, was it 'classified' by the Allies? There was a little red tape to untangle. Fiction must parallel history as much as possible, and that is what is happening here.

“Stranger Associates”

Foreword

This is the second part of a two- book work. The first part is a true story as told me by the inventor of the (stolen) anti- fear drug Hitler called "the drug of the valiant". I was at a training/ sales/international conference at the time and was warned by several powerful people not to repeat it or suffer very dire consequences, so I had to wait at least fifty years. I had half filled a scribbler with notes, etc., from his story told in three meetings/luncheons and as time went on, developed the story from it as the computers improved. The story is as true as he told me, with few embellishments- they weren't needed as you will see- so this part is not long, about 100 pages of readable print. I promised to tell his story some day, including the sequel where his assistant, also a chemist and probably as qualified, but female, and also his fiancé, was last seen shot while escaping Sobibor, a concentration and death camp ordered closed in late1943 by Hitler. Somehow, the inmates found out that all were to be killed when it closed, so they chose when to die with a 'suicide' escape, but apparently 50 survived, however, little is known about who actually did.

Subsequently, the closing of the "Iron Curtain" did little to help clarify things, although a visit from a retired Russian officer, unusual by itself in the sixties, helped somewhat. The whole story was fascinating all through my adult life, and it became a necessity even though I had financial reverses when retired and the industry became 'self-publishing' and took every cent of my meager savings.

Only because of that, the second part may never be published.

This second part, so far, may NOT be true. Even now, 2015 and on, researching is very difficult to sometimes impossible, and if it were to happen it would be a bonus. I will call it a fiction for now, but if Fran were to have survived, and there is no evidence either way, what may have occurred? Could fiction turn to truth? The Russian colonel has helped somewhat, but some events at that place and time were interesting to amazing, and based on my incredible luck and curiosity, and also my fascination at so many personal coincidences relative to the "Strange Associations" story, that this part also needs to be told.

Since this date, some correspondence would indicate I am on the right track.

So many events and stories of coincidences in my life, including people who were present in areas of the events unfolding here, are amazing. This includes, for instance, my close friendship to Marie Tzorak (her married name), the spelling was original, and identical to the name given me by 'Petr". She Canadianized it, dropping the 'T' when they immigrated, she told me. Marie was a young Italian teenager in the early 1950's, mother of a son not much younger than her and a pal to my younger brother, she was married to a burnt-out Czechoslovakian freedom fighter barely able to have periods of insight or sobriety, to qualify as an immigrant refugee family and she introduced me to some of her incredible stories of happenings in Italy, Poland, and the Ukraine. The husband, poor devil, died before the war ended, and is buried in Springhill cemetery. Yes, this unsung war hero, also a hero in "Strange Associations", the true part, became a Canadian next door-neighbor over a decade before the chemist inventor of Valium, a Polish American knowing little of Canada, told me about him! After I picked myself up after "falling off my chair", I dashed out of the hotel to get a notebook to make notes and think of questions to ask Petr.

She told me her son, Paul, was adopted which came as a relief to me at the time. I would like to meet him sometime, she remarried to a Ralph Cameron, so he is either Paul T or Z- orak (or 'C'), or Paul Cameron, and he would be about 75 now, in 2016. Her toughness of spirit (she also survived hell), tenacity, personality, cheerfulness- lived in the moment, cooking, etc., I adapted to the personality changes Fran would have had living through that horrid time. Hence, she had a cheerful, wise, personality and with a very hard, diamond-like core, the mark of a survivor.

Similar items such as these contributed to my choice of title: "Strange Associations", for instance, he mentioned some "crazy Canadians" who spoke French in a similar dialect were chosen to make a raid and door-to-door search for the "enigma" Nazi code machine known to be in a small coastal village in France called Dieppe. They got it, but paid dearly in blood. Their home area, a suburban area of Moncton, New Brunswick, just up the road, eventually had its name changed to Dieppe as a salute to those men, in 1946. I heard about it when the village was incorporated into a town in 1952, at age 14. My colleague with Roche, Raymond Gould, lived in Moncton until his area was amalgamated into the City of Dieppe in 1973.

Many other coincidences are related to my love of, and interest in chemistry, and by a popular concept now: the role chemistry (and all science) has in religion. Anyone has to admit that the human body consists of an infinite number of complex chemical reactions, which, in addition to physics, math, etc., altogether is how human life is. The more one studies pharmacology, the study of how chemicals added to the ongoing chemical reactions-life- works, the closer one comes to explaining life and its beginnings, and the study includes all other studies including genetics. How did it all start, and who, if any, is 'watching the store'? The Bible and the Koran, probably all of these 'How To…' books, are in need of being updated, and by doing this, humans might get along better.

So we have a beautiful, blonde, blue-eyed but ravaged, Jewess surviving WWII but an escapee taking a chance to go east in eastern Europe, a trained chemist unable to divulge it and hiding, but often tempted to use the training to survive and be accepted in a war torn community. So this part I call "Stranger Associates".

1

Redemption

Fran was very cold, which was a very interesting feeling because she couldn't understand why she was feeling anything if she was dead. 'OK, some believe the soul transports to a foetus of another body, and I am submerged in some kind of thick liquid, perhaps it is amniotic fluid'. She thought about this for a while. 'So humans start and end in fluid?

Hmm, not always....I saw lots, thousands, end naked and breathing gas exhaust from the "gasmeister's" engine. In fact, I would have been among them, but I was Max's favourite, and I saw him shot right between the eyes. Yes, he was not in liquid, but his pants were down as he emerged from the men's room. Hmmn...But why am I so cold if I am dead? ...And I am breathing air although I am submerged.....in muddy water?'

She moved slightly and a pain shot through her left side as if a sword is still in her. 'Wrong century....wait a minute!' she thought, 'If I am dead, why so much pain? Am I in Hell, and to look forward to pain forever? Silly girl, I was escaping from hell, don't forget. I remember a bullet going through me, and then fainting, I guess, at least all went black.' Her thoughts were getting clearer...and if I am not dead, and was shot, am I dying?' 'I don't want to die, and that's what they all say, but I do not intend to die! Think of everything I have gone through, that would be a waste, and I don't like waste.'

She touched the hole gently and there was stinging, but not severe pain. The hole seemed to be plugged or blocked some way...and there is an exit hole. 'I think that is considered good,' she thought.

Finally she decided, "OK, I'm alive for now, but freezing in this muddy water (some of which splashed into her mouth as she decided to talk….. to no one! Be careful, it's quiet but let's keep it that way!) So she slithered as quietly as possible out of the ditch, looked around, noticed a lightening in the sky to the east, and was able to stagger to what looked like a river about a kilometer away. About halfway there she stumbled over something that smelled horrible in the early morning half-light, and finally gagged at what was a soldier whose leg came off when she pulled at the pant cuff she had been caught up in. On closer look, there were more maggots than man there, and she gently took the rifle with fixed bayonet from what had been his hands. A soggy bedroll was nearby. "Thank God for you, sir" she murmured as she slinked away with it.

When she got to the river it was too wide and swift to cross, so she found a depression among some trees, lay down with the rifle, covered herself, and found sleep almost before it found her.

The sun was much to the west when she wakened to an odd sound, a sniffing sound, from where? Behind those trees in a clearing, a big, brown dog-very unkempt looking- was doing the sniffing and seemed to be tracking and coming this way. She shook to clear her head and find the rifle, which was empty of rounds. "So this is when I get caught, but I don't see his keeper." She whispered as she strained to look around. The dog spotted her but did not bark as he ran toward her, his ears flat beside his head. He gained speed as he ran with a low growl toward her, and leapt from about three meters away, foam flying from the side of his mouth.

In spite of her knowing it was empty, she pointed and pulled the gun's trigger at him in a desperate reflex, conscious of her weakness, and braced herself for his impact, which would have bowled her over if she had not been standing in front of a tree. The bayonet entered under the jaw, and the stock rammed back to the tree, pushing the blade deep under the jaw and up to the brain. The dog was dead instantly, but she stood in horror for a long time slowly digesting what had happened. Then she fainted, not because she was female- that train had long since left the station- but the loss of blood, not to mention the damage internally, hunger, and the cold conspired against her.

When she came to, she was still alone except for the dead dog. No one had missed it, probably it was a stray. In this time of war, everything dies, it's just a question of when.

'In this era of death and destruction, we humans think only of ourselves, with survival uppermost in mind, and with no thought whatever for the millions of animals caught up in the conflagration,' she thought with sadness, 'I'll bet this dog, someone's erstwhile pet, was half mad with hunger. Perhaps he smelled the blood seeping from my wounds.' Someone more religious might say he, and the gun, and the bedroll, and the muddy hole, and on and on, were gifts from God, but He wouldn't have allowed millions of animals to be caught up and destroyed by a man-made hell,' she mused. Such was her requiem to the poor creature. But, in actual fact, it might just have been a guard dog after its victim, chasing her scent from the prison back in Sobibor, we'll never know.

"Well", she said pragmatically, "I need some protein and iron." So she quickly and carefully built a fire, as she had often done when she was younger and camped a lot, cooked and ate a hind thigh of the dog, destroyed the fire before dark, and walked to the river bank and slept in some reeds.

As she slept she dreamed of recent events, a kind of review taken to another level of consciousness and spawned by her emotional responses, so that the dog had several faces that changed, cruel faces of the worst guards and officers of the various death camps that she had dealt with, and finally the jaded surgeon who had given her a brass ring. His face dissolved into the dog's dying one with the fixed, crooked stare; and then the face of the old chef at her favorite restaurant in Krakow, back when life was good. Apparently, he was born of the rare feeling of a full belly; a similar kind of dream to the one's men get when the vision, albeit extra-conscious, is of a welcoming woman; a "wet dream". The interchange between emotions, recent horrific events, an event of big importance, and resolution on the subconscious, has a huge interest yet to be fully explored. Apparently, it also helps to be wet, cold, wounded, hungry, exhausted, and still alive.

In the early morning, a soft, slow tapping was the cause of her awakening, and on a cautious survey, saw an old rowboat on anchor bouncing against a rock in time with the waves. Looking around carefully, she finally got in to it and quickly laid flat on the bottom praying that no one saw her. After a long period of silence, she peered over the gun whale to see nothing moving, and then she took a chance at raising the anchor, a mossy, overgrown rock, to which the rope was tied. "Hell", she was exasperated with herself while quickly lowering the anchor, as she had forgotten to retrieve the gun hidden elsewhere. Moving as quickly and stealthily as possible, she took the time to get it, watching the quickly brightening sky. Soon under way, she wondered whether she should be going up-, or down-river, also, in one of her infrequent self doubts, whether she should be living at all. 'I developed the habit of living twenty-seven years ago', she said out loud, 'and can't quit now.', and so, over-riding indecision, made for straight across.

On the other side, she was able to break the half- rotted anchor line with a little help from the bayonet ("getting dull", she quipped to herself laconically), and set the boat adrift so it wouldn't be followed. For some reason, it felt like an umbilical cord had been cut; she was in a new country, although in the same war. "Wait a minute," she blurted to no one, "I may need this," and caught the boat as it started to move away, saving it for another day.

I am going to have to stop being indecisive, she told herself, I know it is a feminine trait, but only because men have been given the final say, right or wrong, and women have been trained to accept it. From now on, feeling a bit more confident, I will make one decision after giving it thought, and will live or die by it. Feeling stronger and in control, she scrambled up the bank.

2

Recluse in Ukraine

She had just finished anchoring and hiding the boat in tall grass and rocks on the other side when a Nazi boat appeared, coming around a corner of the river. She dove for cover and was soon hidden comfortably, except for a swarm of insects reluctant to share the space. She mused, 'now I know why they call this river "Bug", in some languages that refers to insects.'

As soon as she hoped the 'coast is clear' she scrambled up the river bank to the relative security of a mossy depression deep into the forest, covered herself with the blanket, so muddy and soiled that it made good camouflage with the assistance of some dead branches, and settled down to wait out the day. Hungry again, she gnawed on a half rotten turnip she had found, missed when a large garden was machine harvested, back near the river. It had a sweet, almost alcoholic, taste, perhaps a little embryonic vodka. Relaxed, but with ears tuned to the most minute out-of-the-ordinary sound, she began another interminable wait.

The bullet holes were dry and crusting, except for the front upper one, sometimes seeping a yellow liquid plus blood, perhaps denoting damage to the gall bladder. She hoped it was beginning to heal, as the others had, on its own. This brought back many memories of the experimental surgeries she had had back in Treblinka (?) or at least one of them. Yes, she thought, it must have been, because Max was my current German officer/protector then. He had objected to a proposed sterilization technique of removing everything including the vagina. In fact, he had the doctor develop some experiments re-connecting muscles in the walls of the vagina so that they would give a ripple effect when his penis was there. Unfortunately, his quest for pleasure gave him the syphilis bacillus I was carrying at the time. Not much was known then about asymptomatic carriers of STDs, and he refused to wear condoms even though the more attractive prisoners were used sexually by up to dozens of soldiers daily. I wasn't completely sure that I was a carrier at the time, but to admit it would have been a death sentence. Therefore, I considered it my 'secret weapon,' a contribution to the war effort. When the problem started to show in his brain, he was transferred, as I was, here. Yes, she remembered, the experimental surgeries done in Sobibor were usually for repairs, and some failures disappeared by dying.

"Anyway," she remembered, "I did not like him in spite of my acting, but I detested him less than the others. He did not complain about the brass ring around my cervix the doctor had installed, probably because he could not reach that far. That was the most painful procedure I had out of the many. The doctor had clamped and pulled the cervix almost out before he put the red hot ring on it, making the pain of the clamp insignificant compared to the burning, I fainted mercifully. I will give this to Max, he gave me some of his opium "Pantopon" pills when I woke up. I was tempted to take them all at once, but got stubborn instead. Looking back now, it was a terrible time, and it changed me more than any other time. I am a hard whore now, and a survivor for me, only. My life with Petr is just a distant dream. When I saw Max shot with his pants down, I took a second to smile; but let's face it, it was a funny sight!" She thought to herself and smiled again.

"Some day, if I survive, I will see about having the ring removed and having normal cycles again in spite of the damage, as much as is possible, and also if possible, eradicating the syphilis," she murmured to herself, keeping her voice low, not only for secrecy, but to timidly explore this so optimistic thought. "Yes, for the first time in a long time, today I am feeling more confident about the future over and above simply survival." And the thought surprised her so much that she carried it like a mental shield all through the night.

When dusk started to make it safe to move, she carefully looked around and she gathered herself for a long hike, moving swiftly and hoping the skies would stay clear for moonlight.

She found herself enjoying the smell of the air on this side of the river. There was much less stench of death, and a freshness in the ground fog, plus a hint of warmth in spite of it being close, if not into, November. It allowed one to try to stretch limits, so she increased her pace east, following a point directly away from the last rays of sun, and then a point obliquely off the moon as it rose. This rudimentary type of navigation kept her path relatively straight through the night, until just before dawn, when the ground disappeared. She fell into oblivion.

Consciousness arrived so slowly that she remained immobile for a long while, going through the now familiar process of awakening and piecing together the realization that she is alive and actually warm and comfortable in bed with only a headache from falling off…..a ledge?....a riverbank? …..a roof! She stifled a groan from habit and carefully opened her eyes. Yes, she was in a nice, warm, bed in a small room, alone…no, a naked man was coming from a bathroom, wiping his very enlarged penis with a washcloth. Am I back in a prison? He must be a soldier, and they don't ever wash before using me, so it must be afterwards. She reflexively touched her vaginal area, in spite of her not wanting to appear to be wakening -and was caught.

"Oh, I'm sorry. I expected you would be out for a while; are you all right?" he said, grabbing for a towel to cover himself. Strange- they usually don't care. Actually, he was blushing, and appeared non-plussed, very embarrassed. After the towel, he donned an old wooly robe, which showed him to be older, maybe 50 to 60, but fit, with the tanned face and body of a farmer, close to two meters tall, about 90-100 kg. and without much stomach- more flat than men of his age, and had a full head of grey hair with a darker beard- no, not a beard, just a couple day's growth. He spoke in Polish, "How do you feel? You were out a long time, so long that I did not think you would catch me relieving myself. I'm sorry, I have not even seen a woman for years, please forget what you saw." "I did not see anything unusual." She said truthfully, starting to feel the pangs of hunger, as usual, but her headache was waning, and the bullet holes were just stinging as if they had been washed. All in all, she felt pretty good, but who was he and was he friend or enemy, and where, exactly, was I, in some kind of cave?

"I have some hot soup for you whenever you are ready. You fell off my roof, you know." He said, smiling and waving a hand, "It's built into the side of a hill, with a sod roof. No one bothers me here." Then he went serious, "Are you in trouble?" he asked, looking at the number tattooed on her arm. She did not answer right away, realizing that she was naked under the sheets and also felt cleaner than she had ever been for a long time. "Did you bathe me?" she asked in answer, "how….?" He cut in, "You were covered in mud and dirt, obviously exhausted, and wounded. I don't often get visitors 'dropping in', and you were very cold, you had me worried." He frowned, "I put you in my bath tub and filled it with warm water. Hope I didn't bother the clots in your wounds, they didn't seem to seep. I did not wipe you, except for blotting with a towel." "Thank you, it feels good." She said, and he continued, "I tried to keep from looking at you." Then he continued,

"You are very beautiful….", he said with a defeated tone.

"Thank you, I appreciate that. Don't apologize, although it feels good and is very welcome, I have not encountered many gentlemen lately and I appreciate your attitude." She said, smiling for the first time in a long time, "May I ask who you are?"

"My name is Dieter, and my last name is not important as it is fake. Poleski will do, if it's used carefully as all tribes hate each other and will kill if your name is wrong for them. This is my home in the Ukraine about 20 km. east of the river Bug, and I am from Poland, as are you. Are you ready to eat? I am able to trade for a chicken once in a while, and this is for you", as he ladled a big scoop of stew with dumplings into a bowl. "We can talk later." Chicken, potatoes, turnip(?), leeks, and spiced with an unfathomable mid- European flavor with fluffy dumplings of potato flour, the most wonderful meal she had eaten for many years, and she told him so every time between mouthfuls. "I have no wine for you, only water, but it is good water… rare nowadays. We can finish with a small vodka, however." And he produced a small carafe with a slightly cloudy pink liquid, and small glasses. "I make it with added beets and leave the color in to hide the cloud…." She had sampled the vodka and immediately fell asleep, so his last words had fallen on deaf ears.

After another deep sleep Fran woke to silence and darkness, but remembered where the candle and matches were, and was soon able to take a good look at her surroundings. The room was larger than she at first thought, with Spartan furnishings and little decorations, as befits a bachelor, or at least a man living alone. But at least it was clean and tidy, as was her clothes, washed and folded on the table; and with a note left for her: "Be back soon, have some business in town. Stay inside and be comfortable, keep lights low. Dieter".

Without going outside, she determined that she was in a man- made cave into the side of a hill, with the hilltop extended to form a roof- from whence she had fallen. The walls were air exchangers, cleverly built, she learned later, to allow fresh air to flow inward when required, but with an exit returning out low, so anything rolled into the 'window' (e.g. a grenade) would be produced out lower at the feet of the attacker. The chimney was well at the back venting at the hidden side of a rock above, with a similar 'return out' vent also sloped to return anything dropped in to be returned at the outside entrance. It drew with two intakes with such force that smoke was dispersed quickly, especially if dry wood was used. A machine gun, fully loaded and braced, was permanently erected pointing at the entrance. This home was, in fact, a fortress, and well disguised with camouflage outside.

On a wall beside the bed was a small framed photo of a group of adults and children, including a younger Dieter in a Polish army uniform. 'Probably his family,' she thought, the woman beside him was very pretty, as was the older one near an older man. Two teenage girls and a much younger boy completed the picture: 'a happy looking group, taken before the war, I'll bet.' I will have to find out how the situation is now, she thought as she replaced the picture. Considering the current set-up she will have to be delicate and tactful, she thought bodefully.

The kitchen side of the room was well equipped with a well and pump, table and two chairs, a counter topped with a well scarred cutting board and homemade drawers under containing cutlery and all the usual devices, plus a rather new stove- one that uses coal (a bucket with charcoal beside it) as well as wood- with a smooth top and a built-in oven, and storage under containing several bread pans and pots. An ice-box was on the other side of the table, with a cooked chicken, raw beef, milk and beer. This was a rich man living very quietly. "I would be as safe here as anywhere," She said to herself, "I wonder if I could stay with him for a while? What could I contribute?"

Hours later, she was still listing what she could offer: 'Obviously, my body although it is limited, and he already wants me. But, there must be more. Security, "two heads are better than one" is the saying. I wonder if I can remember how to make gunpowder as I did back in chem. class? Maybe I can make some matches? Some antiseptics- I worked on one for Roche called Triclosan, it had a number at the time, but it was a new one of a class of quaternary ammonium compounds, I wonder if they ever got to market it?' she thought, 'It was the only one of the group effective in pus or blood, with the new "bis" chemical configuration. I wish I had some now for the bullet wounds.'

As Dieter entered into the house, he was greeted by a naked woman behind the machine gun, asking, "What is the password?" she queried, "You are so beautiful, I don't know!" and he laughed, "That will do," and she slinked toward him with her eyes searching him seductively. "I want you, but it must be different than you know." He was painfully aware that she was watching him grow in his pants, need was pervading all over his body, he had no resistance to her. She was so desirable, and he was so lonesome, yes, that's the word, lonesome. Yes, no one will ever replace my Anna, but if ever they do, she will be it. She is coming closer, but wait, she has stopped!

"I have to explain something to you, dear, I hope you will understand. Many German officers and soldiers have taken me, some doctors have made me have strange surgeries, I am not your average woman. You should not enter me, but I have a strange yearning to swallow your cock. May I please have your penis in my mouth?" she said, dropping to her knees.

He was taken aback. What is this? My god, I need her so badly, but am I clean enough? Will she smell my anus? Those bastards! To do this to this amazing woman, does she really want me to do this? I can't stop! Did I hear her right? She is kneeling before me and unbuttoning my pants! "Really dear, I want to feel you in my throat! Please! Let me love you. I need it."

"My God" He said in shock. Then, as his penis disappeared in her mouth, the impact of the visual shock made him say, "My God", then as her eyes dissolved into bright pools of satisfaction, he said, "My God!, then

"Oh, God", then "Ohhh" as some pre-cum oozed out of him. He then realized he was pumping his cock into her face and could not stop, even if he wanted to. He touched her throat and felt his cock-head moving in it. He pumped harder, and she convulsed in a big gag, but then she took him in again, and her eyes said 'more'. Then he ejaculated with a big groan, and she swallowed harder. He thought, my God, I have never experienced such an orgasm, is she OK? Is she really enjoying this? I belong to her now, she owns my whole cock and now she wants to stuff my balls in, too. She did! Every important part of my body belongs to her. He made a great thrust, and she took everything- he nearly fainted with pleasure! Then a new pleasure overcame them both: an afterglow that was beyond imagination, and they sank into sleep.

Things were now changed irrevocably, and forever. No one had promised anything, but each had promised everything. It was as if a thousand priests had married them for good! No one had said anything. He had not proposed, she had not accepted, they hardly knew each other, and they were together forever! It was as if they had always been together.

In the morning, or maybe later that evening because nothing came from without to indicate what part of the day it was, just whenever they finished sleeping, they became conscious. They had become face to face, with all parts touching each other. No one moved, to move was to destroy the wonderful feeling of togetherness. Petr, no not Petr, Dieter was with her, touching her skin, her breasts, her vagina, all of her with such a warmth that it was impossible to move. His limp penis was lying close to her vagina near her clitoris, she could feel it, it was so close. She remembered it in her mouth and then her throat, making her throat close reflexively, but the feeling of his cock-head ejaculating was making an unimaginably good feeling come alive. "I'm sorry", he said, but she cut him off, "No. Don't apologize for something so nice. I have to explain that I don't want you in my vagina, because it is infected and destroyed, do not use it! I have survived the Warsaw Ghetto, Treblinka, and Sobibor, but I am destroyed. Let me use my mouth and throat to please you, it's all I have left! And I get pleasure sucking you, let me!"

Derek was confused. This strange girl came from nowhere, actually from above as if she was an angel, and now was trying to convince me that she liked having my penis deep into her throat. Maybe she was a dream after all. She might be my wife in a dream, I know she is dead, but she tried that once and she choked. Maybe she came back for another try, NO! That is terrible, don't think that way! My God, I miss her, I would die to be with her again. Is this woman a reincarnation of her? She might make a good partner for now, and if what she says is true she is my ideal sex partner. I must get to know her better. "That is the first time I have ever been so deep in a woman's mouth, and the first time at all for years." He admitted, "I have not been with a woman since my wife. She and all my family were shot when I refused to fight for Hitler, and escaped – well, they called it desertion."

Pointing at the picture on the wall, Fran asked, "Is that your family?" "Was," He answered, choking back tears, "They were cut down immediately by machine gun, no warning, no negotiation, nothing!" "What did they do to you?" He asked her.

"Everything," She said. "I was arrested outside a bank at midday in Warsaw by my own Polish police, yes, Warsaw's finest, for being a Jew, a few days before Poland surrendered, taken away quickly from my fiancé before he even missed me. An old friend of his remembered me as a Jew and gave me up. My fiancé was arranging for a new account as we had just arrived from Krakow, and we were to be married the next day. They questioned me, even tortured me, before they became quite sure I was not a Jew, then they put me in the ghetto anyway. My blonde hair saved me. I inherited it and the blue eyes from my Scottish grandmother. It has been very useful to me."

"While I was in the Ghetto, although I was free but kept in there, it is one big prison with guns pointed inward, you know, and it grew to become one huge prison, so big that others recognized me, non- Jews who had robbed my family. They were there as criminals for crimes other than being Jewish," she said wryly, "and so they gave me up for the second time. 'Misery likes company!'" She mused, then continued, "But the Polish officer who arrested me wanted me for himself, and I refused, so within two weeks, I was sent to Treblinka, but the commandant there at the time picked me out to be one of his mistresses, and I survived the rest. All were gassed, it was horrible. A new gas was tried, they would writhe in pain before dying. In all the death camps there was no mercy. The guards were savages, and the helpers were chosen for their selfishness and cruelty, making them turn into lesser animals." She admitted guiltily.

Dieter looked lovingly at her for a time, appraising her beauty having lasted through all this, then he said, "Yes, those in the Ghetto were trying everything to appease the Nazis and nothing worked. It got worse when some army units counter-attacked, they were annihilated. Then they grouped over a hundred officers of the Polish army under a white flag, and then shot them. An officer of the Nazis then shot them with his pistol in the back of the head, to be sure. That took over an hour." He explained: "I was being questioned by another Nazi officer who was looking for a missing chemist in Warsaw when the report came to him." Then he took a chance to tell her: "I shot him and ran away, eventually to here."

"I want to thank you for shooting him, although it cost you your family and more. I, or my fiancé, was probably the chemist they were looking for. We were partners under a contract with a big Swiss pharmaceutical company to develop a new series of chemicals we had discovered, having an unusual effect on a newly discovered part of the brain.

Actually, we discovered the chemical first, then we traced it to a very old part of the brain, a part of the "nose brain (the rhinencephalon)" in early animal development. A Roche physiologist called it the "limbic system" and reported that it controlled the effect of emotions like fear on the body. The Nazi 'brown shirts', seeing only the word fear, assumed the rest and broke into our lab in Krakow and stole some, which Hitler called an anti-fear drug and gave it to his 'Blitzkreig' troops in the invasion of Poland. He called it one of his 'secret weapons', an anti-fear drug he called 'the drug of the valiant', in German of course. When I tried to find my parents, who were arrested and taken to the Warsaw Ghetto, I went to Warsaw and he came with me. We became separated there when I was arrested. I never saw him again and don't know what happened to him."

"So, we are both on the run. How did you survive?" asked Dieter. She replied, "There is only one way for a female to survive this war as a captive. I was raped by sometimes as many as a hundred soldiers in a week, was pregnant several times, always aborted-so often that pregnancy was more common an ailment than the common cold-, then in Treblinka I was operated on for 'experimentation' like a lab mouse. In one case, they put a hot brass ring around the opening of my uterus to sterilize me. Nearly killed me, but an officer liked what I did in bed and saved me. He had syphilis, I never had symptoms but maybe I am a carrier."

"Well don't worry now, you're safe here, and can stay as long as you wish. I can get some condoms, if I may," he asked with brows raised, continuing, "...and if you wish."

She replied, "Someday, perhaps, it is still too painful to have anyone in there, if you don't mind. Thanks for the option, it's refreshing, I would like to try later. Meanwhile, my tonsils like you." She said, smiling naughtily.

Dieter drifted into thought for a moment, 'this may be a confirming example of adaptation by the body to satisfy one of the three basic needs: eating, sleeping, and procreating. She might be interested in discussing this further sometime.'

He had an overwhelming urge to hug her tight. "Hey, let's have a toast! There is some of my vodka here." He produced a small jug from the shelf under the counter, and a couple of small glasses. "This is a batch from last Spring, wish I could get rid of the aftertaste."

"We should be able to correct that. Off the top of my head I can think of a few filtering processes, and there is something called electro-filtering which involves two electrodes with a low electrical current running through a magnet, I will try to look it up." She said. "I remember the problem was with the electrical conductivity of the liquid, and the chemical composition of the electrodes, and the magnet. Sometimes filtering with electricity causes more trouble than it solves, especially if one is going to drink it. My experiences with Roche, although only under a license agreement for the benzodiazepines, taught me how complex chemical manufacturing for pharmaceutical use is, and clarifying vodka may be a good example."

They toasted and talked, etc., until very late. Other than sharing their individual histories, the only plan made was that they would stay together, and she would explore some filtering processes for his homemade vodka. Then they made love as if they had been married for a long time. He was amazed at her expertise in oral sex, which was something new for him. He was also surprised that his own foreskin was the key element in building arousal as it moved against his erect shaft. Whether his penis was in her vagina or mouth was not as important as how it moved, "one learns something new every day," Dieter thought as he drifted off to sleep.

The next day she helped him in his charcoal-making process: They walked about three kilometers to another cave in the side of a hill with a huge tunnel built for a chimney up to the top. The opening at the top was covered with a porous but strong roof of saplings designed to disperse the smoke in the cave with the help of a number of smaller chimneys creating a strong draft, so when sod was placed to cover the burning wood, making it smolder, charcoal would result. She suggested hardwood only, and of one type only at a time. This would give a more even and inconspicuous taste, if any. Weeks later, his current batch of vodka was vastly improved, and, as it was revealed to her, he was selling it on the black market as usual, but now for more value.

They were now very comfortable with each other, and almost happy. The weather was helping, and there seemed to be a lull in the war. They could almost every night make love in their special way and enjoy the afterglow, then sleep uninterrupted like normal people despite being in the middle of a war zone, and each being "an outlaw with a price on their heads". Things were getting quite normal, that is, on the black market during wartime, with that as the only economy, 'an eye for an eye, a life for a life, and, come to think of it, their vodka was like GOLD.

Snow!.!. White, glistening, beautiful, snowflakes drifting and sparkling in the sun..........and deadly for the duo hiding in their cave if their footprints are spotted. After all, this is the centre of a war zone.

The trees, grass, scars of war, rocks, everything, was covered in a white layer that would make an instant alert if tracks were left. Dieter and Fran were trapped in their own home, but they were ready for it.

One day a pure white rabbit came into the cave sniffing for food and caused a break in the boredom of inactivity while they were capturing it. They had to be silent, but not scare it out, deadly but quiet, capture it quickly. No shots, just a quick blow, but it died loudly as rabbits do. So much for all the efforts at security, so then they had to peer quietly outside for hours, so long that Dieter skinned the dead rabbit and made an up-to-the- minute in fashion hat for Fran. In the mirror Fran said, "It's cute. Thank you, Petr." Then, realizing the error, quickly, "Oh God, I'm sorry.

Can you forgive me, Dieter? This is the first gift I have been given since Petr gave me his ring, years ago." She looked at her missing finger. In an effort to change the subject, she said, "We are equal inventors of the-'pams', but they only gave awards and prizes to men. He gave me it as a wedding ring, because….." and a big lump blocked her words, then caused tears to well in her eyes. Conservation closed. Dieter hugged her, said, "It's all right now.", brushed the rabbit tracks clean and they dined on rabbit stew. They were starting to fall in love.

Although they were stocked up and prepared for a long stay in a very comfortable and safe situation, any disturbance in the snow would betray them, but conversely, the lack of any disturbance would reduce curiosity to nothing. They settled in for a long winter's day. Dieter went to work with his knife whittling wooden plugs, and Fran decided some good, old fashioned, cleaning house work was appropriate, and needed. Each worked at the chosen jobs while Dieter explained that their source of food, in fact everything, was his ability to trade his home-made vodka on the black market. It was the <u>only</u> market. He traded recycled bottles of it with wooden plugs.

When offered a taste, Fran's first impulse was to refuse as she was sewing, but then she was curious about the item that was now keeping them solvent. She had tasted good vodka more than once, in fact, quite often, during the parties the Nazi officers had in the various concentration camps she had known. An involuntary shudder ran through her at the memory. Another involuntary shudder ran through her when she tasted the vodka. With the exception of a strongly apparent alcohol taste- no, not taste- burning effect? It was awful! It was nowhere near vodka, also it was still quite cloudy, perhaps poisonous with a lot of methyl over taste, certainly had a terrible flavor, but gave a nice warming sensation. There was still a lot to do about stabilizing the strength, increasing the ethyl portion, removing dissolved gasses and filtering.

She almost instantly thought of some simple chemical improvements, such as filtering out flavour impurities and some clarifying techniques. To Dieter, after assuring herself she would hold it down and not gag, she asked, "Did you try to clear it?" "Yes," he said, "I used charcoal, but it is hard to make good charcoal here," He said bleakly. "When we are able, maybe I can help you, I was a chemist until the war interrupted everything," she answered.

"Wonderful! I have a lot of competition, and any improvement will increase the value for trade. As soon as we can…."…a distant rumbling sound slowly increased from the direction of a road kilometers away, interrupting their plans for a better situation, and reminding them that there is a war on. "Sounds like some tanks coming, we should get ready," suggested Fran.

"We are as ready as we will ever be, keep calm, you man the machine gun, and I will go over here." He said, moving to a dark corner. They now had no choice but to wait.

After an interminable wait in quiet tension, the sound leveled off, then slowly diminished. Dieter murmured, "Don't relax yet. There may be ground troops," so they waited another hour, and sure enough, a lone soldier came walking warily in the small valley, avoiding the puddles, as it was now raining. He rather carelessly tossed aside some of the branches hiding the entrance to the darkened cave and wandered exactly toward Fran and the machine gun. Her finger tightened on the trigger and she refined her aim, but Dieter quickly came from behind and put his left hand over the soldier's mouth, while slitting the throat with the knife in his right, without stopping, he then stabbed expertly into the chest, then dropped the already dead body. "A Russian," she whispered, surprised. "Doesn't matter, stay quiet." He warned. They waited another ten minutes, and soon someone called from afar, "Yani, where are you? Come on." Then, "Yani, hurry!, then "Yani, come! We are going, catch up!" They heard the calls a few more times, getting fainter each time. "Seems like the Russians are starting to counter-attack, we are going from the frying pan into the fire!", mused Dieter to Fran, she replied, "I hope that's not true," and then, when it felt safe and the bloody snow was washed away, they dragged the body of the young foolhardy Russian to an abandoned dry well, and disposed of him.

"God be with you," they chimed together. "Tomorrow will be another day."

"I just stopped some very complex chemical and physical reactions," said Dieter. "You believe that too?" asked Fran, she continued, "God laid down the laws of nature, the laws of chemistry and physics, and gave each of the elements individual and unique properties- many of which have not yet been identified. Some day we'll learn all of it, but not during our time, I bet there will be lots left to learn centuries from now. Perhaps some day he, or she, will return to view the result." And they went home.

3

Vodka

Increased rumbling of traffic on the highway caused frayed nerves, but there was little seemingly immediate danger, no more wandering, nosy soldiers, or almost anything to suggest that they were in the middle of a war zone. Almost all of the traffic on the highway a couple of kilometers away, was heading west, suggesting that the front line held by the Russians was progressing westward. Has peace finally come to the Ukraine? It's probably too much to hope for, they both agreed, this area has seen too much war in this century. During this few weeks of the lull, they settled into a routine of carefully working on improving Dieter's homemade vodka and reaching the happy state of maximum capacity with increased clarity, due to Fran's 'activated' charcoal.

They were also settling into a happy state of domestic bliss, such as the war would allow them. When Dieter was away, he was looking forward to going back home. Fran, having taken over most of the housekeeping duties, therefore going out less, often found herself gazing out hoping to see her man coming home. Wartime limited everything severely, but one time, Dieter brought her a dress, traded for a bottle of vodka with the local dressmaker under a promise of secrecy of his kinky personal proclivities. When he presented Fran with the dress he almost had to remind her that she was a woman, and a very pretty one at that. This started a big chain reaction with her: she started to wear make-up and lipstick, at least to the extent that something could be found to resemble cosmetics as it would be dangerous for Dieter, known to be single, to buy or trade for some. Dieter traded for a new product called petrolatum, and she mixed in some beet juice to her preferred colour. A darker mixture would provide a type of 'rouge' as shown in the odd magazine, usually American or Canadian from the airbase a few miles away. She even wondered how behind the style she would be from the two and three, year old magazines. Then she found a way to fix her hair in the large rolls now popular. One day she put the whole thing together.

Dieter was preoccupied when he entered, muttering, "BACK" loudly in the direction of the machine gun after he entered, depositing a load of dried firewood on the floor. He froze when he caught a glimpse of a strange, beautiful model from a magazine standing in the middle of his living room. She was tall, maybe 5'7" with blonde shiny hair done in the latest fashion, blue sparkling eyes, with a high colour and full red lips above white shoulders and rising bosom above a perfect figure, small waist, full hips with arms akimbo in a sexy pose, with legs doing without high heeled shoes, actually there were no shoes, and there should be. He could feel something stirring in his loins that he rarely felt any more as triggered by sight alone. He was transfixed, and she knew, and was loving it, feeling like a woman after all these years. This man, feeling like a man, carried this woman, feeling like a woman not since the night years ago before she was arrested, to their bed, and not to sleep.

Slowly, tentatively, quietly questioning his eyes, he said, "Fran..?" Then coming to a conclusion, "You are beautiful." As if to settle an argument among the gods above as to whether the word should be "good" or "pretty" or "Fantastic" or "Gorgeous" or "Amazing" to describe his erstwhile partner in the dirty world of war and survival. For perhaps the first time his helpmate in an almost impossible world had turned into a Goddess. A lump appeared in his throat. He could not say more. She broke the spell with,

"Welcome home, darling". It was the first time she used 'darling', but it fit.

A lot of time was spent in developing a second distilling place, a location only a half kilometer from the first, but in a slightly improved location, still into a hill, but a higher one at the site of an abandoned farm on top with a deep, dug, well that had gone dry. Dieter had already dug into the side a smaller entrance and a bigger, deeper, cavern that connected into the well. They decided to move the charcoal making activity there as the nearly 30 meter well, with an even longer draft, dispersed the smoke already cleaned by some baffles at the rear of the cavern. A searcher would have to work hard to find it, and, with a stroke of optimism and 'greased' palms, Derek had 'inherited' the farm land from long-deceased 'relatives'. Some things are only able to be done in wartime, and then very carefully. It was not luck that seemed to smooth things out, but Eastern European's' love of vodka.

One blustery, snowy, February afternoon both were happily and cosily, putting the finishing touches to their new factory room when an event outside shook the room, causing a small cave-in, broken glass, and a blockage in the chimney-well, backing up the smoke temporarily. "Are we being bombed?" asked Fran. They made a dash for guns and coats, and whatever else they could think of before a cave-in buried everything. Silence. No cave-in. No after shock. They peeked out, nothing. They waited about five minutes, all was quiet, so they ventured out into the small blizzard. Each had a gun, and they agreed to split up and meet on the other side of the hill, carefully but hurriedly as the day was waning early with the help of the snow shower.

They met on the cleared side but saw nothing. Then, as they started up the hill they were met by an airplane wing sliding down the hill, pretending to be a toboggan, it was empty of course, but it reminded Fran of happier times when everyone had toboggans or sleds in her childhood and it seemed as if all of Krakow was laughing and sledding happily. She swallowed hard as the emotion welled up, and she dodged the wing noting as she did that the markings had a very uncommon star shape. It was not German, certainly not Russian or the star would be red, maybe it was American? Yes, she was vaguely aware that the United States had entered the war a couple of years ago. They must be allied with the Russians against the Nazis. Good. I hope they stay friendly after the war, if it ever ends.

Further up the hill the snow squall was passing as if a curtain was opening on a disastrous scene with a broken airplane in the middle and broken bodies scattered around. There had been no explosion, although a bit of smoke or steam was showing from several spots. The plane had gone in nose down about 3 or 4 meters deep. The snow had gently covered all of the horror with a white sheet, a bright white shroud. The plane appeared to have grown out of the ground, then broken.

Dieter's lips were moving silently, and then he crossed himself. Fran felt a tear in her left eye, but that might be caused by the cold air, she thought, as she wanted to be her usual hard, emotionless self. That was a losing battle, and when she spotted the half man still oozing blood into a large pool, she vomited. So much for being hard and cold, she noted, realizing she will never forget this scene even though she had been through worse events.

They found that the same (toboggan) wing had covered the well for a while, perhaps teetered there, then started to slide down the hill according to the track it left in the snow, almost as if it had a mind of its own and ran for help.

The pilot, that is, the person wearing the brown leather helmet and still strapped into the seat, was crushed boneless with the impact. The passengers, five in all, had been thrown, but not clear, at least not alive. Necks were broken, one man was cut in half, one died when the fuselage was crushed with him in between. Except for the pilot, all were in civilian dress. The plane was a B-17 converted for passengers, Dieter observed, and the washroom unit had come off whole, probably because of different welding. A stainless tank with water dripping from its pipe had separated whole. The fuel tank, when tapped, sounded empty. Enough said.

They gathered the bodies and put them in with the pilot, pried the cockpit door closed and hung the dog tags and wallets in a bag on the door, piled refuse against it, effectively blocking out wild dogs or other predators, fashioned a cross, then said goodbye. Dieter retrieved the stainless tank, and they went home. A week later, after a cautious return, the plane was empty, and a note had been left with a single word in three languages:

"Thanks" in English, Ukranian, and Polish.

After stripping the plane and its contents of everything of possible use, Dieter felt like saying in another note: "Thanks, again", but suppressed the urge.

The ten gallon water tank, almost fifty litres, increased the capacity of the fermenting process by about ten times, two of the fuel tanks gave increased capacity for storage of "activated" charcoal, as well as a rudimentary continuous flow filtering system, and the electrical batteries allowed Fran to test some electro-filtering ideas. This all combined to improve the product with clarity and taste, therefore doubling the value (and the price). "With vodka, it is all about the clarity and taste. Price is less important." Both agreed.

They were now really in the vodka producing business, and although they were still dealing with the 'black market', this market was becoming more legitimate not only because it was the only organized one, it was the only one. Many commodities were traded daily without interference from officialdom, because there was no other way. For vodka, as most of the locals liked their vodka, and the product that Fran and Dieter produced, because of its clarity and flavor (or lack), was superior, by far, than any other, the source was becoming legitimate. War can have many effects one wouldn't expect. Legitimacy was less important than availability.

This created a very unusual problem: two fugitives hiding in an unknown place, unidentified as legitimate or otherwise, were providing a common commodity with exceptional superiority, from a secret location, in the middle of a war-not a local confiscation- but a world war- with the front lines nearby, and their business, at least demand, was growing exponentially. What would you do about that?

Fran was troubled about the problem. One little mistake, one little unimportant decision by itself, could destroy what has become both the salvation of them both, as well as their individual destruction. Fran looked at the number tattooed on her inner arm thoughtfully and confirmed her vow not to be taken alive. "Never again," She muttered, "never again." Bureaucracy was developing quickly in the wake of a front in the war which was now moving away rapidly, and the bureaucracy could become dangerous. The clarity, and the purity, of vodka was an issue in what little was left of local politics, which was no more than an excuse to forget the killing happening just a few kilometers away. The mayor of Kiev was making it clear that he was the local power, and that he alone was backed by Moscow. One other distiller was large enough to put up some opposition to the vodka produced by Fran and Dieter, questioning the safety of the methods used to produce this 'superior' vodka. Unfortunately the other distiller was the brother of the mayor of Kiev.

A frontal attack would be useless in this case, thought Fran, no.... something very separate and different would have to take place. After doing a lot of research on her adversary, she found that his wife had been having trouble with malaria, acquired from a trip to the South Pacific before the war. But that is not a problem that should concern us, she is probably taking quinine to keep it at bay. No, I need to find a political weakness to control him, or at least to undermine his charges.

She decided to agree with him. She asked for a meeting with the mayor and his brother to discuss the safety of their respective products, and to set up guidelines for such safety in the industry. That way, the extra ingredients, if there were any, would have to be exposed and tolerable quantities established, as had been the case for a distillation of 'wormwood', a liquor found to be poisonous years ago.

Vodka with juniper berries makes gin, very popular with the British regiment posted in Kiev. The majority use a mix of a water mixed with quinine, making a very bitter, almost sweet, concoction, labeled a 'gin and tonic'. The market for gin has increased with the advent of a drink becoming very popular with the American air force contingent in Kiev, called a "Martini", which is simply cold gin and a little dry vermouth, hopefully vintned in Italy by the Martini company, producing again, now that the war is winding down. Perhaps it is time to expand our product line, thought Fran, now that we are producing 'vodka' so clear, it is really alcohol with a mild fermented potato taste. Electro-filtration and amylase can eliminate that taste change. She decided to try to source juniper berries.

Fran was up early, dressed with extra care, and, primed with research for extra determination, faced the day of the great meeting. Dieter was also well turned out and was armed with a concealed Luger compliments of a dead Nazi officer years ago. This was wartime and one must be careful, but the point of the meeting was to discuss what could be done as the war ended, in addition to setting standards 'for purity'.

The General Administration building was the biggest on the block, and the least untouched by the war- or the best repaired. Guards in uniform stood at the entrance, saluting persons as they entered. The couple were led to a main floor office and introduced to a clerk at the little window to the side. The corridor and hallway was lighted minimally in an interesting way with old fashioned oil lamps, adding to the austerity of the endless walls, and .....Wow! As they entered the small anteroom, as it turns out, the opulence smacked you as if to warn that you were entering a superior establishment. The black leather overstuffed chairs, the high light from a small chandelier, fresh flowers in the vase, mirrors everywhere, suggesting a much larger room. They sat as if to wait, but the guard knocked three times, opened the entry door and announced, "The Dietfran Distillery to see you, sir." "Certainly, show them in." Someone said from far within.

Fran and Dieter entered the most opulent, large, meeting room they had ever visited. The anteroom was just a small taste, this could have been an opulent ballroom in a five star hotel. Three huge chandeliers hung from the ceiling, sparkling excessive light on top of the many oil lamps on the walls, below which huge overstuffed sofas were set diagonally to make points, punctuated with large potted plants. The large meeting table, seating twenty, was somehow dwarfed by the size of the room. Two men sat at the head of the table, neither making an effort to stand, but they did acknowledge the couple. The entire room contradicted completely the austere requirements of Stalin, not to mention the war, but the couple were successful in hiding their amazement.

"I am Gyorgi Stefanovitch, mayor of Kiev District. ('district' was emphasized), and this is Jan Stefanovitch, head of Kiev Distillery." Dieter offered his hand as usual, but none accepted, "This is probably a waste of time," he thought. The mayor was a big, obviously overweight, burly man with the high color of a blood pressure problem. Thick eyebrows, a big nose, and bigger jaw, and grey hair, suggesting age at about sixty years old. The brother was the opposite: younger, but well over forty, with black (dyed?) hair and black moustache, wearing makeup (?), similar to the American movie actor, shorter and slimmer, but with a greasy, untrustworthy, air.

The mayor started right in, "You are making bootleg vodka in my district, and I am told it has impurities." Dieter smiled, only because the expression "bootleg", borrowed from the Americans, sounded ridiculous in Ukranian. "You mean, 'drunk from the boot?' or 'drunk in the boot?', either way there would be impurities, and a strong smell." Dieter answered. This drew a small giggle from the brother, as he swallowed Fran with his eyes.

"This must stop! There will be no unauthorized distilling or impurities in my district." The gruff mayor pounded his fist on the table, rattling the pre-set glassware until one struck the other and broke. The brother looked again at Fran, and then rolled his eyes skyward as a reaction to his brother, or maybe to try to impress Fran. She took the latter reaction and smiled directly at him.

"This has already stopped. You have already received the petition from hundreds of your people demanding our improved, cleaner, vodka, already requested by Stalin himself, and we demand that you rubber stamp your approval. Also, if your brother is to continue to produce his cloudy garbage, it must be filtered first. My wife is a trained chemist who adapted standard filtering techniques to my production, making it the only vodka available here (he waved his hand broadly) without ferric iron salts, copper salts making it green, and rust particles, and God knows what else. Do you want the people who appointed you mayor to die? As for your district, the Germans had 'your district' three weeks ago, and "your people" did not miss your groveling to Nazi generals." Dieter said, pounding the table to answer and copy.

The mayor was non-plussed, he could not speak, no one had ever objected to him as definitely as this person. The brother spoke up, in his slimy way he stood up ostensibly to establish a better presence, he failed. "This is no way to sort out a small problem. I believe we can agree on everything some way over dinner," He smiled at Fran, "may I invite you both to dinner this evening? We could meet here at, say, seven and finish this and the dinner with a nice cognac from the Armanac region of France. As my treat." "Make an agreement and I'll sign it.", Said the mayor, standing up, so as to terminate the conversation.

While driving home that late morning, Dieter suddenly stiffened up and pushed the accelerator to the floor. "We have a visitor," he said, glancing at the mirror and quickly turning into a side street to lose the tail. A big, black Mercedes sped by unwittingly with two men in front, one holding a machine gun, and the brother in back, with the convertible top down. Luckily, the streets of Kiev were winding in this part of town, so Dieter came up behind them so quickly that the driver didn't notice them until too late. The man with the machine gun died with a shot of the Luger, as the last sound he would ever hear. Realizing his quarry was now behind him, the driver swerved but died as he was turning, sending his car at full speed into the side of a building. It exploded in a ball of flame, from which a figure, burning all over and screaming, ran, and then collapsed in a puddle of fire. Dieter resumed his normal speed, blowing on the barrel as he had seen in American movies a long time ago. "You know," Fran said regretfully, "we eventually could have bought him out. Why do people do what they do?"

A few days later, a message was sent to Dieter from the mayor saying, "The Kiev Distillery, now fully licensed, is for sale. We will address all offers."

This seemingly innocent announcement conjured a long, sometimes heated, discussion.

Yes, we were the logical buyers, as Fran had mentioned earlier, and we were prospering enough to consider expanding, but there were many other things to consider including another meeting with the mayor who would not have taken lightly the killing of his brother. Fran was mostly concerned about the safety of another meeting, or the lack of it. Dieter realized that "fully licensed" meant that he was not, and the mayor could shut him down legally if the offer was not addressed; and yes, such a meeting would be dangerous.

They spent all night discussing the pros and cons, and it must be remembered that there was a war on at the moment and even though the United States decided to join the "Allies", as they were now called, Hitler seemed to be unfazed, counterattacking and causing some trouble in the western front, including Stalingrad, and decimating the Canadians who had attacked a small coastal village on the shores of the Atlantic near England, called Dieppe. What were they thinking? So many had been killed in that day, that the Allies would think again about any landing along the Normandy coast. But, of course, any news about the war was just rumor, as the official reports were only propaganda. No one should have to make any long-term decisions with a war on, much less risk their life and livelihood.

Finally, they divided up the problem into several sections: 1) They had to do the meeting, but how to do it and be reasonably safe?[call a town meeting of all vodka users (a festival with free vodka) to publicly discuss the future of vodka] 2) Assuming they met and negotiated, what would they offer, start and finish?[Offer a no charge amalgamation of the two companies as a minimum, or a 'chairman of the board, big salary and pension to the mayor/brother'] 3) After the meeting, how would they escape, or avoid capture or avoid being killed?[the air raid sirens, controlled by friendly Vodka customers, would go off suggesting an air raid, and in the confusion, they would escape in a different car.]

First, they would have to establish a legitimate address.

They talked all night and still came to no conclusions. In the morning, for a start they went each to their normal tasks for the day, her to siphon off their latest batch for filtration, and he to deliver an order of ten liters to a customer as pre-payment for a load of potatoes coming from Liviv. It was about twice the size of a normal load, but they had recently expanded production yet again and had a new cave in which to hide it. Mihalo, an officer fighting with Stefan Bandera's U.P.A. insurgents, had 'liberated' the potatoes from the NKVD there. It seemed as if everyone was fighting everyone in some parts of the Ukraine, so much so that, the world war was almost forgotten. 'Mini-wars' were everywhere.

Mihalo was a tough looking, but a friendly and pleasant, larger man, and the two hit it off quite soon. They were joined by the owner of the restaurant in which they were having lunch to discuss recruiting ideas with Mihalo. As soon as Dieter heard that he was struck with an idea. "Do you have a rear entrance?" He asked. "I have three of them," said the manager, "the freight entrance where you can offload the vodka, another beside it, and a third off to the side. We don't use it much these days, it goes to the side alley and was used more when this building was a movie theatre. The door was nailed shut until an inspector approved it as a fire escape, so now it is only locked from outside."

Discussing the options for recruiting fighters for his insurgency here in Kiev, Mihalo intended to offer free vodka to any Ukranians who would listen to his speeches. At that point in the conversation, Dieter broke in and offered to double the supply so that a 'festival' could be held with free vodka, to 100 ml. each, to the first 50 attendees who were Ukranian. Poles, Russians, etc. would be discouraged, but no one would be barred, which made the owner happy, and he agreed. All excitedly began to draw up some posters: Come Saturday to the FIRST ANNUAL UKRANIAN VODKA FEST, a FREE drink of the new, clear, vodka to the first 50 Ukranians that attended.

The next day Dieter sent a message to the Mayor, inviting him to attend the Festival and speak, as well as to discuss the sale of his distillery privately. They apologized for the duplication of events, but it had been in planning for some time, but on the other hand he would have the opportunity to make a speech as well as make a deal, to 'kill two birds with one stone', so to speak. The rest of the week was very busy: making preparations and advertising to all, delivering the extra vodka, and making plans with Mihalo to be protected if the mayor does anything stupid. On Friday, they were advised that a high official wished to visit the festival and join the celebrations. This added a bit of excitement and worry to the group, as they had no details from the messenger as the message had been handed down over days by several persons. It was more of a warning, perhaps, than an official message.

Saturday morning arrived dark and dreary, hopefully not to herald trouble. Fran and Dieter dressed 'to the nines', then drove a circuitous route so as to enter the city from an unusual direction. She drove pensively, and he checked his trusty Luger, plus a small but long stiletto was taped to his leg. They parked in the alley near the 'fire exit', ready for a quick getaway. They both commented that this felt like one of the American 'Western' movies, with everyone gathering for a 'showdown' soon.

Although they were early, the restaurant was already crowded with some regulars for breakfast, but mostly men and women, young adults, whispering seriously with each other. There was a line-up of people waiting for the bar to open, and two covered tables kept vacant in the center with a podium in between. The mayor was there surrounded by four men who did not smile, with their suit coats open and ready. "Just like a Western saloon" thought Dieter. As a matter of fact, it was, the whole country of Ukraine was just like the 'Wild West', and here the tension was building. Some of Mihalo's friends were scattered around the room, looking tense and wary. Just as the bar was opening, and attention was collecting toward the jugs of vodka, a siren sounded outside and through the front door marched several uniformed soldiers, gathering in a line and saluting at a medium height, rotund man entering. It was a commissar, a high official in the Soviet Communist Party and a native of the Ukraine, Nikita Kruschev. He had a bigger presence than his height, and confidently walked to the podium, smiling. "Hello friends, as a lover of good vodka and a native

Ukrainian I decided to attend this festival. I understand there has been a breakthrough in the clarity of your potion, sir." He announced, addressing Dieter, who signaled the shocked waiter to activate a glass. "People, we are all good citizens of the motherland, except for one dog who has been working against collectivization and against the concepts of communism. We are also here to arrest Gyorgi Stefanovitch, for crimes against the people! Oh, and that is good vodka, nice and clear!" He said, turning toward Dieter and Fran, and then with a lingering look again at Frances, he offered his hand to Dieter, and smiling at Fran asked, is this your wife? "Yes, she is my Frances." Said Dieter, "Very pleased to meet you both." He answered, and Dieter continued, "And she is a trained chemist. She has made significant progress in electro-filtration." "Ah so, very beautiful," He said, looking at the woman, not the vodka. "We should collect all the vodka distillation around the new filtration. Kiev shall be the new centre for progressive vodka!" Kruschev announced. As he took her hand, she made a small curtsy, and said, "Thank you, sir." A veritable agreement among all had just been made, and she had put a period to the statement; everyone smiled and toasted, and Kruschev expounded on the advantages of collectivization in a speech for the next half hour. Meanwhile, the 'mayor' had disappeared, been taken away, and also, some of the friends of. . .and Mihalo, had disappeared! That concerned Dieter, until he realized that his beautiful Fran, as well as Mr. Kruschev, controlled the crowd, and nothing bad would happen. Kruschev would have no way of knowing that Mihalo and his recruits were fighting the Soviet NKVD. Driving home later, Dieter smiled and said to Fran, "That vodka was made from a shipment of potatoes that Mihalo had taken from the Soviet Army." They both laughed at that, and also the nice day that had unfolded, beginning from near disaster. Then Dieter got serious for a moment and said, "No one must ever know that we are Polish, either." And they laughed at that, too.

Back home in bed, thinking of the exploits of the day some more, they realized they were a good team. A team which could withstand almost anything, regardless of the bizarre situation, and also, one in the middle of a war. They were also in good standing with the "powers that be", for now.

4

Wins and Losses

"My God....! He's burning up!" Fran said to no one. After a quick glance around, checking for followers or any observers, she pulled him in and felt his forehead reflexively. A quick check of arms and the left foot showed some wounds, perhaps animal bites, badly infected. Obviously, he had developed a severe case of cellulitis, and could die. She stripped him naked and found a fourth and fifth bite. She immediately heated some water and began to drain and debride the infected lesions, applying lots of salted water. Then she bandaged the wounds and put him to bed, with a cold, wet cloth on his forehead.

She sat down hard, exhausted with the struggle, which may be for naught, as he was in trouble. Already his breathing was a bit off, and his temperature was a way up. What to do?

He really needed a sulfa, which was the golden treatment, but just as rare. She had a little mercurochrome, but it wouldn't last and was useless in the presence of pus. The pus was acting as a barrier, and she couldn't drain it all. Although she wasn't a doctor, she knew he was going to die, unless...no, she did not have the materials to make a sulfa, and the internal risk would be too great. "I just have to keep trying to clean, debride, and drain, to fight the local infection, and try to keep his temperature down. At least he's sleeping or unconscious, and not feeling the pain. I wish I had one of the quaternary ammonium compounds we had worked on before the war, one was especially good in the presence of pus,...I wonder....I have household ammonia and hydrochloric acid in the laboratory in the cave nearby, and can use alcohol for heat- an alcohol flame would be hot enough. I wonder if there is any.....and she set off for the lab nearby, getting more interested and excited as she went over a list of ingredients and processes, as the more she said 'yes' on her mental checklist, the closer she was to making her own treatment. Dieter would be safe for an hour, at least.

Over the next day, hope was turning into frustration. She was able to collect the raw materials or their substitutes, but one process of heating, then cooling, then heating again was not quite working well. The ice was melting too fast. ..and, damn it, it was snowing again...snow! That may be the answer. Taking a chance of being discovered, she picked up the hot test tube with a clamp, put in a stopper, and took it out to a snow bank. Placing it on top of it, she let go and it stuck into the snow and melted its way into the bank to the ground. Within the few seconds allotted, it was cool enough to add an ingredient and heat again. Running inside, she had the ingredient ready, but she couldn't open the tube as the shrunken, cooler air inside formed a partial vacuum, drawing the stopper inside. Finally, taking a calculated risk, she broke the glass tube just below the stopper and hoped the rest of the tube would stay intact,...and, it did! Fran then continued with the experiment until finished. She now had some triclobisonium chloride, something that would have been on the market if the world war hadn't intervened. The Roche marketing people had tossed around a few trade names, such as Triburon or Triclosan, but it was too early to apply them and a number was required for primary research and pre-marketing purposes, but then Hitler overran Poland and all hell broke loose.

As soon as Dieter woke up, Fran began to apply her newly made treatment, she debrided and drained the wounds again, and applied a cream preparation of her chemical, and then wrapped it with a fresh bandage. An hour later the infection in the wound was stopped dead in its tracks, but unfortunately the big problem was in his blood stream where the deadly bacteria was flourishing with only his weakened natural immunity as defense. He still needed a doctor and a sulfa, or that thing that a Dr. Fleming was playing with in England, if there was any truth to the rumors.

Dieter awoke several hours later and, although weak, seemed to feel a bit better, or at least, no worse. They decided to try to make in to the closest hospital in spite of the risks, if he could stand. Also, in weighing the pros and cons, even the physical act of moving, a struggle in itself, would increase circulation and affect the swelling of his ankles. They made it to the car and were at the hospital a half hour later.

Almost immediately, as he was loaded onto a wheeled table, Dieter went unconscious. The nurses could not find a doctor available and were concerned that a sulfa may not take effect soon enough. His temperature was too high, and his kidneys were showing signs of shutting down, but by morning he was awake and able to write a short, but effective will which gave him some peace of mind. Then good luck shone brightly for a short time when a doctor was found, and he, in turn, found some of the new, safer, sulfa called sulfasoxizole with better solubility, allowing a double "loading" dose. But three hours later Dieter had passed. Humans and light bulbs share a similar process near the end: a flare up of light and clarity for a short period before eternal darkness overtakes.

Francesca was devastated. In all of her nearly thirty years, having lived through impossible situations in the middle of a world war, she had never suffered as large a loss as now. With Petr, her lost love, she at least had been free, and her luck had held when she was sent to Treblinka and then when she moved to Sobibor she seemed almost invincible. She had lost a protector, a haven, and an improving life with a man she was starting to love, and now it was all gone, thanks to 'Human' man and his sick wish to overpower and control, even imprison, his fellow man; at least one in every tribe in history has emerged. One man, Hitler, was responsible directly for the death of millions of Jews, Poles, Ukranians, and others, and indirectly responsible for the death and maiming of as many soldiers and civilians worldwide, including her Dieter. Ideas alone have no importance, it is how they are implemented that is. She felt like going back to her cave, and closing the entrance after her. In fact, she did.

Current events and processes keep life living when an individual doesn't want to. Life certainly did not have a good argument for continuing now. She tried a shot of vodka, it was very good but did not solve anything except for putting her asleep soon after. The next day, some papers were left in the door of the farmhouse above her. One was a note accepting the offer placed to buy, or at least to control the other vodka distillery, and an official letter announcing the 'collectivization' of all vodka distilleries in Kiev, to be under the management of 'Mr. and Mrs. Dieter Polsky', and signed by N. Kruschev, Commissar. Interestingly, it was addressed to the farmhouse she had just inherited, so it was less a secret than planned, but it did legitimize the erstwhile 'bootleg' operation. Among the papers was a newspaper with the headline 'Paris is liberated'. This was the only really good news of the day, and Fran busied herself with smoothing out the process of manufacture of more triclobisonium to supply the local hospital at the request of the head nurse. She had been very impressed, and Fran wanted to finish this before she gave up life. She decided to keep very busy and maybe the pain of loss would slowly recede.

With the ever increasing demand for more and more of the new, clear, vodka, and the greater availability of potatoes- the only good thing about collectivization and the positive influence of government- plus the added interest in her more effective antiseptic and the requirement to provide discs of it for the laboratory in the hospital, Fran got her wish to be busy. It was a whirlwind of activity, punctuated by solemn times like Dieter's funeral, then later the burial when the ground had begun to thaw, Fran was too busy to be suicidal.

The hospital boasted two doctors, both women, who were likable but very busy trying to be everywhere at once in a hospital for a city of a million people although, with all the fighting, especially the November devastation, it is a wonder that anyone was left alive. No male doctors were. Certainly few buildings were. All of Kiev was a disaster, and would only be good as a location for filming documentaries and movies about the results of war. Francesca thought about this, as she made her way slowly through the rubble to the hospital, still believing that the human spirit would prevail nevertheless. In two months Kiev was in different hands three times and counting. First the Nazi's, then the Soviets, and finally an army made up mainly of Ukranians who had fought for the Germans, then chased them out of their city, and, without a choice, had to turn it over to the Soviets and the Ukranian communists. There was little left to turn over.

One of the doctors, taking time to say 'hi', said, "Thank you for this, that is an amazing product, did you develop it yourself?" "No," Francesca replied, "it is a chemical under development by Roche. I was doing some chemistry research for them with my hus…my fiancé, when war broke out." She said, feeling for her missing finger. "I am supplying some chemicals from my location here until things settle down. I will try to revert that to Roche if possible, later, as collectivization may prevent that or slow it down." "I'll forget you said that." The doctor had lowered her voice, "it is not wise to comment negatively on collectivization." "Yes," Fran matched the whisper, "our production of vodka may be changed to alcohol as we become larger because of it, and that's good." She replied, raising her voice. She regretfully realized that she was caught up in politics in spite of herself.

Her contacts with the hospital, however, opened a new avenue for help. She found that the laboratory technician was bored with the small amount of work produced for her by only two doctors even though they were overworked. Francesca needed help with setting up a new lab and manufacturing facility she had acquired nearby, now that Dieter was unable to do it. With the help of Mr. Kruchev and collectivization, as well as legitimization, she nevertheless found that the need for a better location and equipment, plus the all important staffing for the other distillery, as well as expansion into alcohol production at different quality levels, and the manufacturing of the antiseptic, would keep her running too hard. She needed help, and fast! She fervently wished, along with everyone else, that the war would end soon. As long as some were still alive, many ex-soldiers would be available as a workforce. Now however, she had to take a chance on anyone.

Sylvia was a 26 year old widow, living in a burned out building nearby. Her husband had been a freedom fighter in Kiev when the Germans had first invaded Kiev after Stalin had changed his mind. Captured shortly afterwards, he was shot in the lower stomach by the Nazis and died in horrible pain a few days later. At the end, he took poison to relieve it. She had a small child and her mother lived with her and could look after it while she worked. The income for a part time laboratory assistant was very low, so she quickly agreed to join Francesca (yes, Fran had dropped the use of her 'nickname of familiarity', as Petr used to call it, in favor of the more formal one) as a part time assistant in the new laboratory, and her income immediately doubled. Francesca also revealed a plan of bonuses for performance, something new she had heard of in the 'new world', which would be paid in the form of partial ownership, or 'shares'- difficult, but not impossible, within the communist system. So long as he was not 'purged', her friend, Mr. Kruschev, would go along with this, she was sure.

Sylvia and Francesca developed into a good team quickly, and much of the heavier work was completed by two handymen originally contracted to build some counters and finishing work in the new facility. One had lost an arm in the fighting, and the other had lost an eye and a leg to an unexploded grenade, and now wore a wooden prosthesis he had fashioned for himself. All men, and many women, were damaged physically by this never-ending war, and certainly every person was affected psychologically, some more so than others. Francesca was feeling very lucky to have gained such a good team this quickly.

With the improvement in her situation came an improvement in the weather. Spring was beginning to show its early flowers and the days became longer. The snow was so dirty with age and the smoke and ash, but it was melting, and flushing away some of the signs of war. Even the wars, yes, wars within war, were quieting into a lull. The resistance movement to the Nazis was winning, the resistance movement to the Soviets was losing, there were minor skirmishes between Poles and Ukranians mainly in bars and taverns, but otherwise, things were getting quiet as if the big war was ending. Perhaps if one were to hold his breath long enough, they would stop.

The partners were very busy now with sourcing of raw materials, and new needs were appearing as a better natural source of sugar for the refined alcohol was beets and they were scarce. Also, they had to source two acids, hydrochloric and hydrochlorous, as well as laboratory grade ammonia, from out of the country. The work was getting intense.

In May 1945, the allied forces announced that the war in Europe is over. They didn't say which one as the rest of the world thought there was only one. Keep holding your breath here. Then a gang raided the potato warehouse, killing the guard, a nice, friendly man with only one leg and eye. Surely there was no need to kill him; for a few pounds of potatoes? People are very hungry this Spring in the Ukraine, and it might get worse as there are few whole people remaining in this war-torn land to rescue farmland from neglect and decay, less with any tools or machinery to cultivate it, no livestock to restock it, few distributors, fewer stores-with empty shelves of course, and no one here to run the show! Therefore, because of the communist doctrine of collectivization there was little incentive to repair a land you did not own. Despair is dissolving into famine.

5

Pogroms and Prisons

Fran was running out of potatoes. In 1944/45 winter, potatoes were hard to come by in the Ukraine, or Poland, or anywhere near the war zone. Everyone was fighting everyone as if that was a substitute for eating, and maybe that was right, because there was no food and people were starving, so the Poles blamed the Ukranians blamed the Jews (if there were any left) blamed the Germans blamed the Soviets blamed the Poles. Then follow the circle again.

She –they- had done something about it starting in late 1943, by developing a better machine for mashing and peeling potatoes, by peeling then mashing the potatoes. Since it is a 'trade secret' and patented as well as one could in the Ukraine, the 'process patent' could not be divulged; i.e, there was none. Suffice to say that peelings and all went into the 'mash', but at different times for clarity. Also, the item that was added at a stage when cloudiness was a problem, would make you nauseated. But there was a by-product that was still nutritious, and a good food for the newly discovered vit-amines and for minerals and ash (now called fibre), and they would dry it, finely ground, as a sort of flour. In fact, they called it 'potato flour'. Bags of this 'potato flour' was appearing on shelves in the 'black market' beside the ersatz coffee and ersatz sugar, which was a mixture of beet sugar, dust, sand, and saccharin, as developed by a pharmaceutical manufacturer in the 1930s. Sometimes this 'potato flour' was the only real food in the whole store! There was a little yeast, so dumplings, pancakes, and close relatives of them became popular. But I digress, Fran was running out of potatoes, and she had already tried substituting other starchy tubers like turnips and some varieties of radish, but one can only use a small percentage of them. She needed potatoes.

Dieter decided to make a trip to Lviv. Maybe he could find another truckload like last time. The Ukranian National Party was still fighting the NKVD and was gaining ground mainly because the Polish regiment of the Waffen SS was deserting the Nazis and joining the Ukranians, their historic enemy, against the Soviets which was a more disgusting option, but the best at the moment. Someone had heard that a ring of adversaries was closing in on Hitler, so we could return to our old enemies for the comfort of enjoying familiar enemies for a change.

In Lviv, Dieter was making it known that he was interested in 'big lots' of potatoes in return for vodka, a message that would reverberate in the rumor mill, as vodka was actually more scarce than was food, and seemingly more important. His daily routine was to visit some bars and taverns all over the city so as to cover as many factions and sub-factions as possible, then contact a couple of different contacts at the end of the day. He was in conversation with so many people in so many taverns, that inevitably he was drawn into an altercation just after he had found his supply of potatoes and was relaxing with a good beer. A bump on his right elbow sent his beer flying into the décolletage of a busty woman laughing with a big, burly uniformed man. As the beer soaked into the two well rounded globes, Dieter's head was rocked by a blow to his jaw. Shaking his head to recover, he felt his wrists enclosed by handcuffs, and another blow put him out.

He awoke in the Lonskoho prison. They had taken him to the regular city jail for processing but could find no papers on his person, just the Luger but it wasn't loaded so they put it back, however someone identified him as a Ukranian citizen from Kiev. That man overheard the police saying the jail was full, so some had to be sent temporarily to 50 Lonskoho Street. A small groan went up from the group as no one had ever left that prison alive. The onlooker had some potatoes and a terrible thirst for good vodka, so he decided to make sure that a message got back to Dieter's friends.

Dieter dazedly looked around, fingering his bruises, trying to make sense of his surroundings. Obviously, he was in some sort of prison with bars on high, small windows but each person was in small individual cells locked with a deadbolt. The room containing the cells was locked, he supposed, and on the other side a stairway was blocked with heavy, old, chicken wire. The smell was ungodly, if he didn't know better he would think he had died and gone to Hell. He tried to separate them: urine and feces of course, vomit....old vomit, sweat- but dirty sweat, there was no sign of a shower, or come to think of it, no sign of anything modern, like the set of a play he had once seen called "The Man in an Iron Mask" by Alexandre Dumas who wrote "Three Musketeers". His head ached and he was hungry, or nauseated, -couldn't decide which. An antique bench was hanging from the wall by two chains, just like the set. He picked himself from the floor and laid down. The floor was more comfortable, and he slept on it, shaking off dread about how long he would be here. A rat skittered across the floor, wishing him 'Good Nite!'

In the evening, a bowl of thin, lukewarm soup and a holely, mouldy, old blanket was passed in from the outside through the bars in the main room, soon night closed in. The place was so dark it was light-as his eyes became adjusted to the darkness moonlight shone into the room from the high, barred, windows. After he got bored with trying to figure out what happened: big round but wet breasts, then nothing; he noticed writing and engravings on the very old walls. It wasn't new grafitti, one stone had a date, July 13, 185? The last digit was unclear, either a six or a zero, hard to tell, and had been engraved by maybe a small knife or spike, or.....? There were sayings in many languages, and two words would describe the feeling: forlorn to final. He was in an old- fashioned prison. Hope they didn't forget him.

Days went by with no break from the smell, dampness and dankness, and the hunger to the point that he was sure the gruel he was passed improved every day and became slightly gourmet. 'If I'm here much longer I will go crazy!' So, they came and let him out. Apparently, a friend in Kiev was a friend of a minor official but with a rising star, a Mr. Kruschev. The others were kept.

The next day a group of NKVD soldiers came to the prison and emptied it, taking every one, maybe a guard or two as well, to the Janowsha work camp in the north of Liviv. It seems that now that the war was waning, other wars and battles were draining the Soviets of materiel and food, and they decided to create some rather than take it. Maybe it was because there was nothing left to take. With that news, Dieter went weak with shock, because no one ever leaves that place alive. They either die of overwork or hunger, but they die without ever leaving.

When Fran received a message that Dieter was in prison, she started to realize how much he meant to her. She knew a mistake had been made, or an event out of his control had put him in this predicament, as he was usually so careful with his movements. She didn't know how serious it was, they couldn't add any more than that he is in prison. In this kill or be killed atmosphere, no one can afford to be in the least compromised. Although they had lived closely together for well over a year, and they had survived a few mishaps and adventures, they had concentrated on the secrecy of their environment and survival as escapees from all factions, that they had never considered each other as more than partners in the business of surviving. Fran now had very strong feelings for her man.

Sometimes it takes a serious event to bring true emotions to the surface, and this was one such serious event. "I am worried about this man, my partner, perhaps for the first time." She told herself, perhaps not really believing it, but definitely feeling it. "Will I ever feel his strong, rough, hands on me? Maybe I will never see him again, ...No, I can't let that happen. I think I have fallen in love with him, or maybe it's a strong dose of lust. I miss him. I miss his voice, his jokes, even his smile. What will I do?" She pondered.

Next day a strange associate showed up. She had just finished a delivery to the busiest tavern in Kiev, and when she was leaving, the older minor politician she had met recently was entering. "Nice to see you again, Madam." He said politely, looking her up and down impolitely, but tipping his hat. She smiled, and decided to return the look.

"Hello, Mr. Kruchev, how are you?" She said boldly, and he said, "I was about to have one of your clear vodkas, will you join me?" "I would be honored to, sir." She agreed, as he led her to a table in a corner of the room.

After a series of prolonged exchange of pleasantries, an aura of flirtation developed, which she suddenly changed by saying, "I have a problem which seems insoluble, probably even you cannot help me with this one." "What is that, my dear?" He replied, "What would you make you so sad?" Referring to the small tear she produced in the corner of her blue eye. "My partner went to Liviv to obtain more potatoes for the vodka and somehow found himself in prison by mistake and has now disappeared from the jail he was never in." "They have lost track of him. It is a bureaucratic problem, as he was arrested on suspicion, and sent to the jail there, but he was never booked in, and he did not escape, he is lost!" "Leave it to me, I can fix it." He said, taking her hand in the two of his, "I will call Liviv now, and make them find him!" He smiled.

A couple of days later, Dieter appeared at her door, and fainted.

6

The War is Over

FROM THE FRYING PAN.....

Yes, in May, 1945, World War II in Europe has ceased. Japan has decided to fight to the end, but that end is nowhere in sight. The Allies, including England, Canada, United States, Australia, China, and many others, have focused on Japan, and regardless of some activity in planning reconstruction and re-division in Europe, Japan gets most of the attention. A meeting is called of the "big three", but just Stalin and Churchill show up to discuss what will happen in Europe. Churchill makes a list for discussion called a "Naughty List", and they sort out who goes back to where. The powers that be move people around to re-settle and re-develop many Eastern European countries. Before Berlin is divided, many, as much as 75,000 Germans, are sent to Poland and the Ukraine, overloading a broke country with refugees who are broke. Nothing makes sense during this immediate post war period.

Petr's Fran, now our Francesca Louise Poleski, the acquired name for 'respectability' as a notable resident of Kiev, Ukraine, and head of the city's only Vodka distillery and also a blooming medical supplies distributor, wakens this morning to a beautiful, sunny, Spring day. She lingers and daudles in bed, savoring the feeling that she is now free and in charge of her own destiny, she has friends in high places-always a necessity, but now unique in that everyone is fighting each other. It is no longer a question of ethnicity, but more like tribalism, no one trusts a neighbor much less a friend. She remembers the friend of Petr's and how surprised he was when he caught the 'friend' attempting to turn them in at the beginning of the war. This started her thinking of her erstwhile fiancé, "I wonder if he survived the war? So few did that it is difficult to imagine how he would as an Einstein look-alike, he looks like- no, he's probably gone- looked more like an intellectual Polish Jew than I do." She thought, touching her missing ring finger. Out loud, she said, "My God, how I miss him", she swallowed hard and got out of bed.

Petr stayed in her mind as she got ready to go into town. How old would he be now? Did he still like strong tea in the morning? Did he still like animals and birds, and visit the park in Krakow, or was he even there in the old city any more? I will never know, my chances of seeing him again are less than nil. Now that the whole world is in a terrible war, does he still have his chemist's philosophy? When man cannot count on man any more, should he count on a ethereal being? Something beyond understanding? Not simply chemistry, physics, and math? Petr would often say, "I know what I know." "I hope he is still alive," She said to no one, as she got in her car. Her brass ring was hurting, as she drove away, "I will get that out soon", She promised herself.

On the way into the city, she narrowly avoided a disturbance on the main thoroughfare. It seemed to be a parade, but with no music, a large crowd had gathered, so large that she couldn't see so she got out of the car and pushed forward. The crowd was jostling and difficult to get through, all were focused on the people marching, with No Clothes! They were all women, bruised and cut, patches of hair-scalp- were missing, they were made to march like Nazis, a knee-high kick and then stomp, all were crying, some getting sick, or stumbling. The comments and the spitting and kicking meshed together so that it took some time for her to realize that the crowd was berating the women marching to their death as collaborators and sympathizers. She quickly returned to the car and backed up, hoping not to be noticed. An old saying surfaced, "There but for the love of God go I", and she shivered as if a cold ice cube were sliding down her back.

Her first thought was to stop the car and stop the people from doing something stupid, but then she realized she would be doing something stupid and she might be 'requested to join the ladies'. So she did nothing, and that hurt. "Will this killing never end?" she said out loud, and through tearful eyes, she almost collided with the answer. With a quick right turn, more of a reaction than a conscious thought, an old jeep full of soldiers wearing the red star narrowly missed her, and it couldn't stop because another truck full was too close on its heels. In less than a minute all hell broke loose into a rattle of machine guns and a few single shots in return. Soon all was quiet again, and she found she was speeding recklessly without realizing it, getting away from another horror. Later, she found out that the soldiers cut down the citizens, who were mostly Poles, and "rescued" the women, although some had been killed along with the onlookers. Still later, a bulldozer came along and dozed them in a mass grave, cleaning up the area.

Shaking, but quickly calming down, she decided then and there to move away from the Ukraine-Poland area, far away. It would be her life's work from now on, and also it would be her life saving work. She had survived many narrow escapes, too many to lose now that the war is supposed to be over. Life has no value here. Then she met a man who had a very interesting approach to life, and to the Jewish race. A Frenchman.

In Kiev, after a frustrating afternoon trying to source potatoes in a country on the verge of famine, she found herself having one of her own vodkas in the best hotel in Kiev. She was proud of the clarity and even the shine of light through the sparkling glass, although she knew why it sparkled and wondered if it had been well rinsed. "These new soaps called detergents must be well rinsed, even one molecule left will destroy the head on beer, the nose on wine, and the delicate taste of vodka." She mumbled to herself, as she often does these days. Suddenly, a male voice with a different accent cut through her reverie like a knife. "Are you talking to me?" And her mind woke up to a handsome man smiling beside her, with a sincerely confused, questioning, look on his face.

"Oh. Hello. I was just thinking out loud," She retorted, "didn't realize I was talking out loud, too." She was talking with a man in his forties, dark, with one of those attitudes of devil-may-care that give him a perpetual shrug, and eyebrows continually questioning, but those strong shoulders are not moving even though his eyebrows are. "But it's not a problem that can't be solved?" he questioned. "Oh, not a problem," She answered," I was just thinking that if these new detergents are not rinsed well from the glass, the vodka can be made less attractive." He was silent for a while.

Then, "Do you know me?" He asked, searching his mind for something to remind himself. "No, should I?" She retorted, wondering why he is taking this line of approach. He finally visibly relaxed, and, with a quick laugh, said, "I thought you might be talking business, with the talk about serving soapy drinks here." Then he said, "…they are, you know." And he offered his hand, "I am Pierre Louis Rothschild, et vous?" He said by mistake, switching languages habitually.

For the first time in a long time, she gave her full name, maybe to give it competitively to his, ".. And I am Francesca Louise Poleski, owner of the local vodka distillery." With that he nearly fell off the stool, "Really?" Then, "I own a vodka distillery in France," with that he shifted his weight a bit too much, falling, and catching himself quickly.

With a smile, a laugh, and a toss of her head, she said, "Have you been sampling your own product?" nodding towards his difficulty with the stool. "The shock and amazement is unsettling me, I did not expect to meet you this way. I have come all the way from Paris to meet you," he retorted, trying to gather his senses, looking at her with obvious appreciation but trying to hide it, trying to be debonair and failing, hiding by ignoring the sexual attraction, therefore failing at all efforts at composure, he continued, "and here you are. An amazingly beautiful woman who has made this most amazing vodka." With that, he offered his glass in a toast. Clinking her glass, he smiled, looked deeply in her eyes, and recovered all at once the control of the scene and maybe her, as she felt a warm, very almost forgotten feeling in her lower belly.

"Goodness, it is just good vodka," she replied, "surely, there are other 'amazing' vodkas in the world." He held the deep glance, saying softly, "None so than yours," but he might as well have been saying, "none so than you", because that was what she was hearing.

At that point a waitress appeared, breaking into the conversation and breaking the mood with, "..will you be staying for dinner? We have some fresh caught seafood this evening, with the chef's seafood chowder to begin."

A raised eyebrow from him, and a slight nod from her settled the question, and he added,

"Yes, can you bring a wine list, a celebratory bottle of champagne is in order. Do you have anything from Rothschild freres?" Again, forgetting the language slip.

By the time the chowder arrived, they were as comfortable with each other as if they had met years ago, and the staff had a sense that they were serving an historic event. Pierre was describing the huge estate holdings he and his brother had in France in vineyards and wine from their family, but he wanted to make and sell the best vodka in the world. Vodka, he believed, was most underrated because its potential had not been recognized as a base for a multitude of mixed drinks as yet, and growth was exponential for mixed drinks, especially in the U.S.A., which was becoming, or appearing to be, a rich country. The clarity and purity was paramount, and he had heard about the differences she was introducing.

"What led you to develop such a breakthrough in filtering?" he asked, needing to know the answer, but wanting to progress to more personal items.

Fran wanted to progress to more interesting things, too, but as she had to start from before the war, many remembrances were making the story grow. "Before the war, we were a couple of chemists having a lab in Krakow with the university there. We developed a five sided carbon ring stable enough to test pharmacologically, and a big pharmaceutical research company in Switzerland brought us under contract. They used a process for clarifying using bentonite, a clay with an unusual particle size, so that was my first experimenting in filtering, and we tried it in vodka. The second was my own, using electricity in an opposite way to electroplating, I have the patent."

"Yes, we use the bentonite for clarifying wine, but it also helps the yeast while fermenting, by swelling and making cozy little caves to house the yeast cells and keep them happy. Happy yeast cells make more happy yeast cells, happier wine, and the world goes around." He tried for a suggestive mood, but never knew if he succeeded. Maybe it was too subtle. He was smitten, as was she, but they paid attention to the meal as it was being served, with civility and small talk, as if they appreciated it.

However, by the time the champagne was finished, a deal was struck whereby she would move her factory to France and combine it with his, assuming it would be allowed to leave- Mr. Kruschev would have a say in that,- and because his brother held the purse strings, it would be called something relating to his love of a pure strain of geese similar to the Canada goose, a near perfect member of the strain. Otherwise, it was, as they say.

"Good to go."

THE END

7

Acknowledgements

My first book, "Strange Associations", was told to me by the main character, Petr, of course, so the notes in a quickly purchased scribbler was the backbone, supplemented by maps from Google.

The second part, a fictional sequel to Fran's attempted escape from Sobibor, as described by the Russian retired Colonel, a fellow escapee who was able to visit Petr after the war, a feat in itself, is my attempt to explore what may possibly have been impossible: The survival of an attractive, Jewish woman alone in a war zone forest travelling on foot, wounded, east toward the Ukraine in October, 1943.

My main acknowledgement is a heartfelt thanks for the minute detail provided in the book, "Savage Continent" by Keith Lowe. He has done a fantastic, thorough job, and I congratulate him in his ability to make my job so much easier. When I began this project as a retired pharmacist with a big empty hole in his life after losing his soul-mate, my enthusiasm quickly deteriorated when I found a dearth of information about Poland and the Ukraine as the Iron Curtain closed tighter with the 'Cold War'. Everyone had a different opinion, no one had facts, until I found Keith Lowe. Thank you, Keith. Also, writing about a period much later, Tim Judah confirmed many things for me in his work,

"In Wartime, Stories from Ukraine", thanks tim.

Printed in the United States
By Bookmasters